Hermie
and Bernie

By Stephen R. Mueller

PublishAmerica
Baltimore

First printing

All characters in this book are fictitious, and any resemblance to real persons, living or dead, is coincidental.

PublishAmerica has allowed this work to remain exactly as the author intended, verbatim, without editorial input.

ISBN: 978-1-4489-1813-3 (softcover)
ISBN: 978-1-4489-9393-2 (hardcover)
PUBLISHED BY PUBLISHAMERICA, LLLP
www.publishamerica.com
Baltimore

Printed in the United States of America

Contents

CHAPTER 1: The Adventure Begins 7

CHAPTER 2: A New Home 12

CHAPTER 3: Split Up 18

CHAPTER 4: A Round for Bernie 21

CHAPTER 5: The Tournament 30

CHAPTER 6: Not Quite Yet 37

CHAPTER 7: Hermie's Front Nine 41

CHAPTER 8: The Second Nine 53

CHAPTER 9: The Tournament Ends 68

CHAPTER 10: The Display Case 75

CHAPTER 11: Found at Last 81

CHAPTER 12: The Comeback 86

CHAPTER 13: A Nine to Remember 96

CHAPTER 14: The Playoff 111

CHAPTER 15: The Reunion 118

Hermie
and Bernie

CHAPTER 1
The Adventure Begins

The sky was bright and clear as the sun peeked over the horizon. A new day was beginning in the city of Merryville. It was time to open its sleepy eyes and greet the new day. Merryville, a small town on the east coast of the United States, has a population of about seven thousand people. Many of them work at a large business on the east side of town called Elite Manufacturing. This facility manufactures all types of golf equipment.

Elite Manufacturing has been in the golfing business since the early 1960's. This year Elite is coming out with a new line of special golf balls. The golfing community is eagerly waiting in anticipation of this new line. There's high expectation.

The new line of golf balls would have the EXCEL logo stamped on them. These golf balls would have a special dimple arrangement and be soft-covered. All golfers would benefit by their use. These balls though are especially suited for use by professionals because of their compression and durability. Two of these special golf balls are what this story is about. Their names were Hermie and Bernie.

Hermie and Bernie began their journey into the golf ball world as a small solid rubber core. They each were then tightly wound with one very long rubber band fiber. With their fiber secure they rolled further down the assembly line. In the next special area there was an extremely bright light overhead. They stopped on a rack. There they were covered with a soft-covered cover and sprayed with a safety coating. They stayed there for what seemed a very long time and then moved on.

Hermie, Bernie and the other balls then stopped below what seemed like a gigantic press. They were about to receive the most important thing of all. They would be stamped with the Excel logo and number.

Hermie looked over at Bernie and said, "Bernie, we're both going to be Excel number one balls."

Bernie excitedly responded, "We should have an exciting life ahead of us wherever we go. At least there's a good chance we will be together for a while."

Hermie and Bernie rolled further down the assembly line where they were cleaned and polished. Hermie looked around at the other golf balls and wondered who else had the Excel logo number one.

Now, it was time to get packaged for shipment. The balls were packaged in sleeves of cardboard and clear plastic with three balls all of the same number. Hermie and Bernie were packaged with another Excel One ball. He introduced himself, "Hi. My name is Arturo. What's yours?"

Hermie answered, "Hi. My name is Hermie and this is my friend, Bernie. It looks like we'll be traveling together. Do you have any idea where we might be going?"

Arturo told them, "I don't have any idea at all."

From the sleeves the three balls were transferred into clear plastic boxes of twelve containing three of each number. The final step was into the master carton where they were sealed, addressed and moved to the shipping dock for shipment.

The shipping department was in the back of the factory. There were numerous cartons labeled on the dock for destinations all over the United States and the world. The carton with Hermie and Bernie inside was placed on a specific pallet with the letters AZ above it. Hermie and Bernie had no idea what their label read. All they knew was what the label read would be their future home.

That night the golf balls rested nervously in their cartons. They all wondered where they might be going. Hermie smiled over at Bernie and said, "Bernie, at least we're going to the same place." Bernie just winked at him. All the balls talked among one another. They all wondered what the courses and players would be like. Their imaginations began to run quietly among themselves. It would be a restless night on the shipping dock.

The next morning couldn't come quickly enough for the golf balls. Hermie and Bernie had beads of sweat running over their covers. Inside the carton there was nervousness, excitement and anticipation. Finally, a warehouseman with a forklift approached the pallet that had the carton Hermie and Bernie were in. He lifted the pallet and moved it towards a truck when he was stopped.

A man with a clipboard approached and told him, "Be sure you load those cartons for that special delivery in Arizona."

"I was just about to load them. They will be on the tail end of the truck. That's one of his first few stops, right?"

The man answered, "Yes, according to the manifest it should be his third stop. Thanks." With that said the pallet was placed onto the truck. A few more cartons were placed next to them on the truck as well as some other golf accessories. The back door of the truck was then shut and locked. Soon they would be on the road to their new home.

Hermie looked over at Bernie. He whispered to him, "I wonder if that is where we're going?"

Bernie asked Hermie, "Do you know where Arizona is?"

Hermie told him, "I have no idea. I guess we will just have to wait and find out."

John, who was going to drive the truck, told the dispatcher, "See you in about ten days." The dispatcher bid him a good safe trip. Shortly thereafter the engine started to rumble. There was eager anticipation among the golf balls for what may lie ahead.

Hermie and Bernie where thinking about what they had heard when another golf ball in the carton interrupted them. A voice said, "Hi, my name is Richie. What's yours?"

Hermie answered, "My name is Hermie and these are my two friends Bernie and Arturo."

Richie said, "Hi. I see you have an Excel logo like me

except a different number. Do you know where we're going?"

Hermie said, "I heard the driver talking about a golf course somewhere in Arizona."

Bernie asked Richie, "Do you know where Arizona is?"

Richie told him, "Arizona is in the Southwest United States. It is very beautiful, warm and the sun shines almost year round." Then with all three of them listening attentively, he continued, "I had a friend who went to a golf course in Arizona. If this was the same course, you will enjoy it a lot. He told me the course was in a valley with mountains on both sides. It had tree-lined fairways and numerous water hazards. Many tournaments were played there year round."

Bernie asked Richie, "Do you know what happened to your friend?"

Richie told him, "Last time I talked to someone who knew him they said he was a range ball somewhere. I'd be with him be I was kept back to become an Excel ball."

For the next four days all the golf balls in the carton listened to what Richie had to say. It made the time at least seem to go by faster. Day after day the truck went on, stopping only twice to open the back door and unload a few cartons. Finally, on the morning of the fourth day the truck stopped and began to back up. I was early in the day but you could already feel the warm sun beating down on the truck. The back door opened and there stood John and another man. Could this be it?

CHAPTER 2

A New Home

"Well, it looks like a beautiful morning." John told the man next to him.

"Yes," he said, "we've had wonderful weather the last few months." His name was Harvey. He was one of the club professionals here at the Ambassador Country Club.

The driver told him, "I'm John. According to the manifest you're getting about twenty cartons."

Harvey said, "Let me get a two wheel dolly from the pro shop. I'll wheel them right into there." Soon he was back and the two men began to unload the boxes. Hermie and Bernie were in one of the boxes they chose. Harvey made about six trips before all the boxes were in the pro shop.

John told Harvey, "That should be the last of your shipment. I'll be in shortly to help you verify it after I secure the rest of the load and lock the back door."

Harvey said, "See you inside." and off to the pro shop he went.

Inside the pro shop Harvey found the packing list and began to unpack the cartons. He said to himself, "All right, the new line of Excel golf balls. They're here just in time for the upcoming tournament scheduled." He just finished unpacking the first stack of cartons when John came in.

John asked, "Anything missing so far? I'll help you finish unpacking the rest of the cartons before I go." It took about thirty minutes till they were finished.

Harvey then spoke, "Thanks for your help, John. It looks like the shipment is complete according to the packing list. Al, the head pro at the club, will be especially happy that the Excel balls arrived with the shipment. We both thought that they would be backordered." Harvey then gladly signed all of the necessary paperwork.

John said, "Thanks Harvey and I'll see you next time. Say hello to Al for me. Sorry I missed him this trip."

Harvey said, "I will and you have a good day and a safe trip. Good-bye and thanks again."

After John was gone, Harvey moved some of the new supplies into the storage room. Hermie and Bernie out of their main carton were among them. Their anticipation of being used would have to wait a little longer.

The storage room was dark and dreary. Two light bulbs and a small window provided the only light. From the clear sleeves Hermie and Bernie could see there were different brands of golf balls, shoes, bags, gloves, clothes and other equipment on various shelves. There was even baskets of range balls neatly arranged on shelves. Harvey put the new equipment in the middle of the floor. I'm sure he planned to put it on shelves later. What Hermie could see of the room it seemed quite crowded.

Hermie asked Bernie, "I wonder what shelf we will go on? It looks like all the golf balls go over there."

Bernie said, "Maybe there will be a special shelf or area only for Excel balls."

Arturo interrupted Bernie, "It looks like all the golf balls are shelved together over there by the window."

Richie then spoke up saying, "Of what I can tell and see this might be the club where my friend had gone to."

Then one of the range balls on the shelves heard Richie and spoke up. He said, "My name is Arnold. What was the name of your friend?"

Richie told him, "His name was Harry."

Arnold told Richie, "I believe your friend is over there."

"Harry!!" Richie excitedly said.

"Hey, Richie." blurted out another ball. "I'm over here in the second range basket on the floor."

Richie saw where Harry was and his rubber band fibers tingled with excitement. He couldn't wait to talk to Harry to see what had been going on and happening. The first thing he noticed after seeing Harry was that he had a red stripe around him now. He asked him, "What happened that you became a range ball?"

"Well," explained Harry, "about three months ago I was bought in the pro shop by an elderly man. While playing the ninth hole with some friends, his tee shot went into the woods on the left side of the fairway. I never saw him again."

Richie gasped, "What happened after that?" The other

golf balls in the room listened intently to what Harry said next. Everyone else was silent as Harry continued.

"I was lost in the woods for about two months." Harry told them. "Finally one day a young boy found me and brought me to the assistant pro, Mr. Jacobs. He cleaned and shined me. He then painted a stripe on me and I became a range ball. I was fine with me for then most of the time I only get used when there are tournaments at the club."

Richie and Harry kept talking for hours. Hermie wanted to talk to Arnold. Hermie introduced himself. "Hi, my name is Hermie." he said. "I just arrived here today."

Arnold said, "Hello, Hermie. Welcome to the Ambassador Country Club here in Tucson, Arizona. The other golf balls and I heard that some new golf balls were arriving soon. The club is getting ready for a major tournament. We heard the caddies talking about while they were cleaning us."

Hermie wanted to find out more so he asked Arnold, "How long have you been here at this club? Do they have a lot of tournaments here?"

Arnold replied, "I've been here for over a year. It seems that a tournament of some type is held here every couple of months. I was first used by a touring professional here at the club. Then during a practice round, I was hit into the water and lost. Eventually, I was found and turned into a range ball pretty much like Harry and others."

Hermie then asked, "It seems that whenever a ball is lost and then found they become a range ball. Is that always the way it is?"

Arnold said, "It seems that way. It's not all that bad. At least you get used and get to meet other golf balls like you."

Hermie then asked, "What do you know about the golf course and the Ambassador Country Club?"

Arnold gave him the run down. He explained, "The club is nicknamed "The Snake". The reason is the way it slithers through the trees and can grab you at any time. It is a stress test and highly regarded in the golfing community. The club is private. It is used exclusively by members except when a tournament is held. The golf course is a par seventy-two track measuring just over seven thousand yards in length. Well-trapped with over one hundred bunkers, the fairways are tree-lined and there are a few lakes strategically placed. Every hole presents its own challenges. Every hole will reward a well-played shot but penalize a wayward one. The golfers call it a formidable challenge whether it's a tournament round or a regular round."

Bernie then asked who was listening as well, "What is the head professional like?"

Arnold told them both, "His name is Al Hart. He has been in the golf business for over thirty years with the last ten years here at the Ambassador Country Club. He's easy going and has a very pleasant disposition."

Bernie asked, "Is that the man who helped unload us off the truck?"

"No. His name is Harvey Jacobs. He's the assistant pro here at the club. He has been here for about six months." said Arnold.

"He seems like a nice guy too." observed Bernie.

Arnold kept on talking about the happenings at the club.

Hermie started to daydream about what type of golfer would select him from the case. He wondered if it would be a professional. He wondered if he would eventually be a range ball like Arnold. He wondered if he and Bernie would be bought together. So many questions unanswered.

"There's an upcoming professional event coming soon to the club. I think that's why they were so excited when the Excel golf balls arrived. Many of the golfers were looking forward to using them." Arnold told Hermie and Bernie.

"When is this upcoming tournament?" Hermie inquired.

"According to one of the caddies the professionals should be arriving this week for practice rounds. The tournament starts in about a week or two. About one hundred and sixty golfers are expected to play four rounds over four days." exclaimed Arnold. "This is a very prestigious event to win for any pro."

Hermie looked over at Bernie and said, "This could be our chance to get selected by a touring professional."

Bernie, with a tear coming from his eye said, "I hope we get selected together."

Hermie said, "That goes for me too."

CHAPTER 3
Split Up

Hermie and Bernie had been at the Ambassador Country Club for about a week. They had been moved from the floor to a high shelf. From the high shelf they could see the entire closet. Hermie and Bernie so far had spent their entire time in the storage room. During that time Al and Harvey had been in and out of the storage room several times. Other golf balls and supplies were taken from the room but all the Excel balls remained untouched.

A beam of light shone through the window and the storage room lights flicked on. Mr. Hart opened the door. He looked around and picked up some gloves and baskets of range balls. One of those baskets Arnold was in. A short time later he came back again. He picked up more range baskets and left.

A third time was the charm. Al came back this time with Harvey and told him, "Lets' setup the display for the Excel balls. The players will be looking for them." Harvey told him, "Okay. They're on the top shelf next to the window."

A new adventure was about to begin for Hermie and Bernie. With anticipation of finally getting used on a golf course, both of the golf balls rubber band fibers began to expand with excitement. Mr. Hart first placed the golf gloves in their display next to a big display case. He then started with the golf balls. He said to himself, "I should place the new Excel balls in the tray in the front of the display. That way the players can see the new Excel balls have arrived."

Harvey interrupted Al, "Would you like me to finish setting up the ball display for you?"

Al said, "Thanks, Harvey. Make sure you put the Excel balls up front."

Harvey put Hermie and Bernie in the front tray of the display case. Harvey had put them though a few balls apart. In fact Arturo and another ball were between them. Being apart from his friend made Hermie realize that they could get chosen separately. He may never see Bernie again. This made him very uneasy and sad. He thought to himself, "Maybe they would get lucky like Richie and Harry did and see each other again." Time would tell. It took Harvey about another twenty minutes to finish the display for the golf balls.

It was a sunny warm day at the golf course. The golfers were just starting to arrive. The players, while their caddies waited outside, came into the pro shop to either register for their golf game or to buy the supplies they needed. Al and Harvey were both behind the counter to help them.

"Good morning, Jim." said Al. "Are you playing a practice round today to get ready for the tournament?"

Jim replied, "Yes, I have a tee off time at nine o'clock. I'm scheduled to play with the two Anderson brothers."

Jim Jackson was one of the better golfers at the club. He was a stockbroker but still was able to practice or play every day. He had been the club champion for the last three years. For the upcoming tournament he was going to play in, he had received an invitation from the club for being its defending champion.

Jim then told Al, "I need some golf balls and tees. Have any ideas?"

Al suggested, "How about trying the new Excel ball. It just came out and is suppose to have high reliability and durability."

Jim said, "Okay, pick me out three of them and some tees." With that Al reached into the display case and took out three Excel balls and three bags of tees. One of the balls was Bernie. For the first time in their lives Hermie and Bernie were really apart.

Throughout then rest of the day Hermie remained unsold in the display case. It was lonely there without his friend. Even Arturo, the other ball he had been packaged with, was gone. He was one of only a few Excel balls left in the display case. He would have to wait and see what the next day might bring.

CHAPTER 4
A Round for Bernie

With Hermie separated from his friend for the first time, a new adventure for Bernie was about to begin. Jim left the pro shop. Outside he met his caddie, Charlie Duggan, who had carried his bag before. They went to the putting green to get ready for the morning round of golf. With Bernie and two other balls in his hand Jim began to practice putting.

It was a warm day at the course. The sun beating down on his cover felt good to Bernie. The blades of grass tickled his soft cover. It was the first different sensation he had had. The tapping of the putter on his cover was gentle and the rolling over and over made him woozy. After a short while he started to get used to it. Shortly, thereafter, Jim stopped and rested Bernie and the other two balls in his hand. Being to late to go to the range, he walked over to the starter shack where he met his playing partners and their caddies.

Jim said, "Good morning, John. Good morning, Bill. It

sure looks like a nice day for a round of golf. All three men then exchanged handshakes and walked over to the first tee.

At the tee their caddies were waiting with their golf bags. At the Ambassador Country Club they only use caddies and have no golf carts. Charlie had been a caddie at the club for almost ten years. The other two caddies, Josh and Richard, were new to the club but had caddied before elsewhere.

John then asked, "Who wants to go first?"

Jim said, "Why don't you and Bill go ahead and tee off. I'll tee off last." Jim gave two of the balls to Charlie. One of those was Bernie. Charlie put them inside the bag, pulled out a glove, a few tees and zipped up the bag. Bernie would have to wait a little while longer to get used.

Inside the bag Bernie got to talk to some of the other balls and tees. He asked one of the balls, "Do you know what Jim is like? He's getting ready for the tournament? Have any of you been used by him before?"

One of the balls, who had some scuffmarks on him, spoke. He told him, "I have been in the golf bag for about a week. Jim used me before and he did very well. I was used for only the three finishing holes. That's why I'm here instead of the shag bag. Usually he uses you only once and then he puts you into the shag bag. I see by your cover you are an Excel ball. Jim usually buys new balls only when he's going to play in a important tournament Maybe we can talk more later. By the way my name is Archie."

Bernie said, "Nice to meet you Archie. My name is Bernie."

Anticipation of being used in a tournament made Bernie

feel tingles inside. It was what he and Hermie had often talked about. If only he could tell Hermie about it.

Jim was doing quite well that day. On the sixth tee Jim was two under par and decided he would change balls. He told Charlie, "Pull out one of those new Excel balls. I want to see what they react like."

The caddie pulled a ball from the bag. It was Bernie. He was about to experience what a golf ball comes into the world to do. The caddie tossed the ball over to Jim. The sixth hole at the Ambassador Country Club was a difficult tree-lined par four with water all along the left side of the fairway. Jim set Bernie on a wooden tee and the caddie handed him his number one wood.

Bernie was getting excited and had many thoughts going through his mind. He thought, "I hope I don't end up in the woods. I wonder if the impact of the club will hurt. I wonder what it will be like to fly through the air." All these questions Bernie asked himself would soon be answered.

Jim addressed the ball getting ready to make his swing. The first swing gave Bernie a breeze but that was only a practice swing. With the wind slightly behind him, Jim addressed the ball, took a deep breath and started his backswing. Bernie braced himself for impact. Then with perfect timing Jim started his downswing and impacted Bernie.

Bernie grimaced with pain and "OUCH!!!!" he blurted out. He then realized he was flying through the air. He opened one eye and observed, "It's beautiful up here. It's like being a bird. Up here you can see the whole course, the other players and even feel the warmth of the sun more."

Bernie flew for nearly two hundred and fifty yards before impacting the ground. He bounced a couple of times and rolled another twenty yards before stopping.

Bernie would now have to patiently wait for Jim and his caddie to arrive. He thought to himself, "At least I avoided the woods. It sure was great flying through the air. I look forward to doing that again and again." He had a special tingle in his fibers. He then wondered if Hermie was still in the pro shop or would he ever get to tell him what this feeling was like. He really missed his friend.

Jim arrived at where Bernie was laying in the fairway. He looked over at Charlie and asked, "How far do you figure we have to the pin?" Charlie told him, "To clear the sand trap in front its about one hundred and forty yards and another five yards beyond that to the pin."

Bernie braced himself for another impact. After a short discussion Jim decided what club he wanted to use. Jim made another smooth swing and again Bernie flew through the air. This club impact didn't hurt Bernie as much as the first one. Bernie flew straight, over the trap and onto the green. He made a small divot when he hit and spun backwards a few feet. He finished about ten feet from the pin and ended up with a big clump of mud on him.

Charlie tapped Jim on the shoulder acknowledging a well executed shot. Arriving at the green Jim repaired the divot and marked Bernie with a coin. He threw Bernie over to Charlie to clean him and began to line up his putt. As Charlie cleaned Bernie the towel tickled making Bernie giggle. Bernie was soon clean again.

"Great putt, John." exclaimed Jim after John rolled in a long double breaking putt from about thirty feet for a birdie.

"Knock your putt in as well." Bill urged Jim.

Jim replaced Bernie where the coin was. He lined up the putt from all angles and sides. He told Charlie, "I think it will break slightly to the left. Is that how you see it?"

Charlie whispered to him, "That looks good to me."

With a pure stroke Jim gently tapped Bernie and he rolled smoothly across the green on the intended line. They had figured the line correctly for Bernie dropped right into the cup. It was a birdie. It was a great start for Bernie and a great hole for Jim.

All three players with smiles on their faces walked over to the next tee where they would face a difficult tree-lined par four. In the past Jim had found the trees more often than he cared to mention. Jim would have the honors so he teed off first. He placed Bernie on a wooden tee and selected a one wood. Bernie again braced himself for impact. With a deliberate and well-timed swing Bernie went flying into the sky with both eyes open.

"Ouch!!" Bernie blurted out. The pain subsided quickly as he realized he was flying through the air again. The wind felt wonderful against his cover. After a short flight he hit the ground in the middle of the fairway about two hundred and seventy yards from the tee. He rolled another twenty yards before he finally came to a rest. Both of the other players hit their tee shots in the middle of the fairway as well but not quite as far as Bernie.

Bernie waited for Jim in the middle of the fairway. While he waited, he listened to the birds chirping and the wind howling through the trees. It finally gave him a chance to introduce himself to the balls the Andersons were using.

"Hi. My name is Bernie. What's yours?" he asked.

One of the balls answered, "My name is Arthur and my friends name is Archie. We are Armor balls. I see by your cover you're one of those new Excel balls."

Bernie said, "I've only been here for about three weeks. I couldn't wait to get out on the course."

The balls kept on talking till the players arrived. John was first to hit his second shot. It landed on the green some forty feet from the cup. Bill was not so lucky as he found the greenside bunker. Talking with his caddie, Jim selected an iron for his shot. Jim made another smooth swing but instead of flying straight at the green, Bernie veered to the right. He landed half-buried in the same trap as Bill hit into.

Jim told Charlie, "I pushed that one slightly."

Charlie concurred and said, "It was the right club. You will just have to get it up and down for a par."

Jim said smiling, "You know that is why I like you. You're always thinking positive."

When Jim got up to his ball in the sand trap, he saw that Bernie was half-buried in the sand like in golf terminology, a fried egg. His next shot would require all his skills and an explosion shot with a delicate touch. This kind of shot wasn't familiar to Bernie. It made him a little nervous and scared. Jim dug his feet into the sand to get a firm footing. With a delicate touch and a strong swing Bernie and some sand popped out of the trap like a cork out of a bottle. Bernie landed on the green gently and finished only about five feet from the hole. Bernie breathed a sigh of relief for it was over.

What an experience and what a story he had to tell the other golf balls like his friend Hermie.

"Great shot, Jim." said Charlie. "Now lets get the par."

Bernie was proud of the shot Jim had executed. Bill made a good sand shot as well. With John two putting, all three players were able to make well-earned and satisfying pars.

The next hole that the threesome would face would be a tricky par three. It had three sand traps with one large one in front. There were two small sand traps to the right. To add to the fun a steep slope in back of the green would catch a shot hit too long. There was a small pond short of the green to catch any really muffed shots. If the wind blew from the east, the hole was one of the more difficult holes on the course.

Charlie asked Jim, "Do you want to change balls?"

Bernie began to sweat as Jim answered, "No, I'll wait till we finish the ninth." Bernie let out a sigh of relief and wanted to hug Jim for his decision.

Talking it over with Charlie, Jim selected a club. He placed Bernie on a shorter wooden tee. A smooth well-timed swing and Bernie flew through the air. He flew high and straight at the green. He landed with a thud and generated quite a large divot. He spun backwards towards the hole but stopped right on the lip of the cup. It was a nearly perfect shot by Jim.

"Great shot, Jim!!" Charlie excitedly blurted out and gave him a high five slap.

John, Bill and their caddies all acknowledged the great shot. Bill told Jim, "That's a keeper." Jim thanked them all. John and Bill hit their tee shots onto the green as well but not as close as Jim. All of them walked together talking back and forth about their shots and the upcoming tournament. Bernie was lying there so proud of Jim and he wished he could express it. Jim tapped Bernie into the cup and gave him a little smooch. Bernie seemed to blush.

Jim then told Charlie, "Sure glad we didn't change balls." This made Bernie feel like part of a team and he played a major role. It made his dimples tingle with exhilaration.

John and Bill lipped out their birdie putts and had to settle for pars. So it was off to the ninth tee. The finishing hole on the front side is another difficult par four with trees all the way down the left side. Jim had the honors so he placed Bernie on a wooden tee. Little did Bernie realize a new chapter in his life was about to begin.

Jim prepared to make his golf swing when a strong breeze came up. He still made what seemed a good swing but instead of flying straight and true Bernie veered to the left. Bernie flew into the trees. He clanked off one tree, veered father left and hit still another tree. He was deep into the woods. It was dark and spooky. Bernie wished he could yell out and tell Jim I'm over here but he couldn't. All Bernie could do was to see if Jim and his caddie could find him amongst the trees, branches and leaves. Twenty minutes went by which seemed like an eternity. Jim had not found him. Bernie, lying there among the twigs and leaves could hear Jim and Charlie talking.

Jim said, "Well, I guess that ball is lost. I'll have to play my provisional."

Bernie began to cry and his heart sank. Bernie said to himself, "I may be here a long time. I probably won't see Jim again either. It sure is lonely in these woods. I wish Hermie was around so I had someone to talk to. Hermie could always cheer up any situation." Bernie remained unfound in the woods the rest of the day.

CHAPTER 5
The Tournament

Bernie was lost. Hermie had no way of knowing the nightmare his friend faced. It was what all golf balls fear. Being lost and your future uncertain made Bernie sweat with nervousness. He wondered how many days, weeks or months he would be alone in the woods. All Hermie could do was to hope his friend was fine and pray to see him again. He had been doing that since Bernie was gone.

Meanwhile, Hermie was still inside the display case in the pro shop. It had been a long lonely day for him with all his friends bought and gone. Many golfers came into the pro shop that day, but only a few of them needed any new golf balls. As Hermie laid there in the case, he dreamed of the past. He thought of all the fun he and Bernie had joking and kidding around back at the assembly plant. He wished Bernie was here so he could tell him about the course and what his day had been like. If Hermie only knew what had occurred.

Mr. Jacobs was getting ready to leave for the day. He decided before he would leave to restock the display case so it would be ready in the morning. It was going to be a busy day at the club tomorrow. Hermie remained where he was in the case but new golf balls were put all around him. He decided to talk to the ball next to him and said, "Hi. My name is Hermie. What's your name?"

The ball turned towards him and in a deep nervous voice said, "Hi. My name is Jeremy. I see by your logo you are an Excel ball as well." Jeremy continued to talk non-stop. "I heard there's a tournament about to start. Sure hope we see some action in it. Have you been here at the Ambassador long?"

"I've been here about three weeks. This is my second day inside the display case. I heard also a tournament was about to begin." exclaimed Hermie.

Jeremy kept on talking a mile a minute. Hermie and Jeremy had come from the same factory in Merryville. He had arrived in the recent shipment with other Excel balls. Most of his friends were still in the closet. Some of his friends ended up at some different golf courses.

Hermie interrupted him, "I had a friend Bernie who was bought earlier in the day. I haven't heard from him since. I hope he got used on the course." Jeremy told Hermie, "You'll be lucky if you ever get to see your friend again. Then again funny things do happen on golf courses." With that Hermie went to sleep but not before praying for Bernie and to see him again.

The night went by fast and before they knew it morning had arrived. The sun created a rainbow shining through the windows. You could feel the warmth of its rays. The front door was unlocked and in walked Mr. Jacobs with a quick step to his walk. He seemed to be in more of a hurry than usual. He checked the register, verified tee times and quickly straightened around the pro shop. It was as if he were starting to get ready for something special.

A short time later the door opened again and in walked Mr. Hart. Al then asked Harvey, "Is everything ready for the big day? I see by looking outside that they finished the final touch ups on the big scoreboard last night. It should be a great day for a tournament and the weather looks good throughout the weekend." With the hearing of that Hermie along with Jeremy realized what it was. The tournament was about to begin. Would all their prayers and hopes be answered by being part of a professional golf tournament? Time would tell.

It was about six-thirty. Many golfers were checking in at the pro shop. Most of them just registered for their tee time and picked up a bucket of range balls. There was a lot of excitement and anticipation in the air.

One of the golfers approached the display case. Al said, "Hi, Jack. Welcome back to the Ambassador. What can I help you with?"

His name was Jack Hammer. On the pro tour for about eleven years, he had won fourteen tournaments in that span of time. This tournament a couple of years ago, he played four of his best competitive rounds of golf. He went on to win the tournament by five strokes. Jack really enjoys the sport and the competition.

Jack said, "Hi, Al. How have things been going for you? I believe I have a 8:40 tee time this morning."

"Let me check the sheet." said Al. "Yes, you do and you are playing with John Taggert and George Pullmer. I see by the sheet they both have registered already. Can I assist you with anything else?"

Jack answered, "Yes, I do need some golf balls and tees. Thanks for asking."

Al then inquired, "Any particular brand of ball you prefer? We have the new Excel balls as well as the new Accuracy balls. Which brand would you like?"

Jack pondered and then decided, "I'll take six Excel balls and three bags of tees. I also need a bucket of range balls."

Al pulled six Excel balls including Hermie from the display case. He also chose Jeremy. They both had been bought. At least Hermie was with a ball he somewhat knew. Jack left the pro shop, put the balls and tees into his golf bag and went over towards the starter.

Jack said, "Richard, nice to see you again."

Richard, who had been the starter for a number of years, said, "Nice to have you back at the Ambassador, Jack."

The starter shook the hand of Jack and told him, "I would like to introduce you to Donny Mitchell who will be your caddie over the four rounds." Donny came on over, introduced himself and picked up the golf bag.

Donny was thirty years old. He had been a member at the Ambassador Country Club for about fifteen years. He could read greens very well and had caddied previously in the tournament. Donny with the bag on his shoulder and the bucket of range balls in hand asked Jack, "Ready to go to the range? Mr. Taggert and Mr. Pullmer are over there now."

Jack said, "Yes, lets go over to the range and get limbered up. We can talk to the other players when we see them on the first tee." With that said Jack and Donny were off to the practice range.

Inside the golf bag Hermie along with Jeremy made some new friends. They introduced themselves to a variety of tees, gloves and other golf balls. There were also some old scorecards and pencils in the bag. Hermie noticed one of the scorecards were from the town he was born, Merryville.

Then one of the golf balls spoke up, "Hi. My name is Archie. Welcome to the world of professional golf."

"Hello. My name is Hermie. This is my friend, Jeremy."

Archie then explained, "Since you're the new kids on the block, I'll try to explain what's going on. Jack is a professional on the tour. He plays in a variety of tournaments around the United States and Europe. We travel with him and do the best job we can do. Here at the Ambassador he has won this tournament once before. I'm still here in the bag because I was only used a little in the last tournament. Eventually, we all end up in the shag bag."

Jeremy then inquired a little nervously, "This is a tournament we're about to play isn't it." With sweat rolling over his eyes Hermie reassured Jeremy everything would be all right. Jeremy then whispered to Hermie, "I've heard rumors of golf balls getting lost in the water or woods and never being heard from again. Doesn't that worry you?"

Hermie told him, "Those aren't just rumors. They

happen quite often in a golf balls life. Our life is full of hazards and unexpected trouble. You just have to face them."

Archie then told Hermie and Jeremy a little bit about the tournament that was about to begin. He told them, "The tournament is held here at the Ambassador yearly. You play four rounds over four days with the lowest accumulated total winning the tourney. After two rounds there's a cut and only about half the field plays the final two rounds. A win here is a plus on any golfers resume."

Hermie then asked Archie, "How do you know so much?"

Archie told him, "I hear caddies talking and I have been in this bag for over three months. In that time I have talked to a lot of balls and other equipment."

With Hermie and Archie still talking inside the golf bag, Jack began getting ready for his round of golf. He had a specific routine he followed on the range. It usually took about forty-five minutes limbering up and practicing a variety of shots. He would always hit the last five balls with his one wood.

When Jack was done, he and Donny walked over to the practice putting green. Donny took three balls out of the bag. One of them was Hermie. Hermie was about to experience his first golf action.

Jack practiced putts from a variety of distances. The putter touching his cover was exhilarating and made Hermie feel alive. Hermie rolled smoothly across the surface of the green. Plunk! into the cup he dropped. Donny took him and the other two balls out of the cup and tossed them back to

Jack. A few more putts and Hermie was back inside the bag. It was time to start the round.

Hermie told Archie, "That was kind of fun putting and rolling on the green. Who do you think he will use today?"

Archie answered him, "I don't know but I'm sure we'll find out soon."

CHAPTER 6
Not Quite Yet

It was going to be a warm day for a round of golf. The temperature was already in the high eighties. The wind that there was had a slight breeze coming out of the west. It would make for a difficult and challenging round of golf for all.

It was time for Jim and Donny to go over to the first tee. The other two players and their caddies greeted them. Jack shook each of their hands and said, "Hi. Looks like it should be a great day for a round of golf. Good luck to all of us."

John Taggert answered, "It's nice to be playing with you and George again. As I understand the course hasn't changed much. Hope we do better than we did last year." Last year all three of them missed the cut after two rounds.

George Pullmer greeted Jack as well saying only, "Good morning and glad to be playing with you again."

All three caddies knew each other from playing at the

course. Ironically, they had all gone to the same school and played on the golf team together. Donny said, "Hi, Jim and Joe. It looks like we meet at the course again."

The starter then announced, "Will the eight forty tee time please report." With that announcement John, George and Jack were off to the first tee. Their caddies with their bags were right behind them.

On the tee the players exchanged scorecards since in a tournament you aren't allowed to keep your own score. The starter then announced, "Mr. John Taggert from Topeka, Kansas is up first. Will you please tee off."

"I'll be using an Armor six ball." he told George and Jack. It's always appropriate to tell your fellow competitors the type of ball you're using to avoid confusion. John then hit a solid tee shot straight down the middle of the fairway in perfect shape.

The starter then announced, "Now on the tee, Jack Hammer from Miami, Florida. Will you please tee off."

Jack then got a club, ball and tee from Donny. He didn't select Hermie. He would have to wait a little while longer. Jack then stated, "I'll be using an Exactor four." With that he took two practice swings, addressed the ball and launched it into the air. It landed in the middle of the fairway in perfect position for his approach.

The starter then announced, "The final player for this tee time is George Pullmer from Los Angeles, California. Will you please tee off."

"I'll be using a Pilot three." he told the other players. Then he took two practice swings and launched the ball into the air. It veered to the right and ended up in the rough. It was the shortest drive of the three.

The three players with their caddies walked off the first tee to a nice applause and a good luck from the starter. For the next five hours Hermie remained unused in the golf bag. He spent most of the time talking to Jeremy and Archie who weren't selected either.

Hermie asked Archie, "Who was the ball that Jack had selected?"

Archie told him, "His name was Cal. He was one of the Exactor series balls. He always seems to have a chip on his shoulder. He thinks he's better than any other ball."

Hermie inquired, "Do you think he's jealous of all other balls or just some?"

"I suspect he's more jealous of Excel series balls. The Excel series came right after the Exactor series. Cal often wished he had been one of those special Excel balls. I'm sure he will gloat when Jack puts him back into the bag after the round." said Archie.

After five hours had passed by when Donny unzipped the bag. He dropped Cal and some tees inside. The round was over for the day. All the balls, tees and gloves were interested to see what Cal had to say.

"Hi everybody." Cal said. "Jack played very steady the complete round. He had no bogies the complete round but did make four birdies. It gave him a score of sixty-eight. It was the lowest score in the group by two strokes."

"Didn't he have trouble on any of the holes?" one of the balls asked.

Cal answered, "On the seventh hole he hit me into the woods but found me right away. He still made a miracle par on the hole sinking about a forty-foot putt. On one other hole he almost made a hole-in-one. He really played great."

Hermie then inquired, "Why do you think you got chosen?"

Cal told him, "In the last tournament he used one of my friends and did quite well. He must have been hoping the luck would continue. Aren't you one of those new Excel balls? I left the factory just as they were going into production."

Remembering what Archie had told him, Hermie answered, "Yes-s-s-s."

Cal then told him, "Since I'm the last Exactor in the bag, you may have a good chance of getting selected tomorrow. I suspect I'm on the way to the shag bag after this tournament is over."

Hermie said excitedly, "Do you really think so?"

Hermie would now spend another day and night away from his special friend, Bernie. Hermie began to wonder where Bernie might be. Would he ever see his friend again? Hopefully, he was all right and their paths would luckily cross again.

Meanwhile, the whole day Bernie had remained unfound in the woods on the ninth hole. Many people had been in the woods that day but no one saw Bernie amongst the leaves and branches. He hoped and prayed he would be found eventually. It was lonely and scary in the woods. Bernie would often dream about his friend, Hermie, and wonder what he was doing. He also thought about Jim Jackson and the wonderful experience he had provided him on the golf course. It looked like still more long days and nights for Bernie in the woods.

CHAPTER 7

Hermie's Front Nine

The next day brought bright sunshine and a beautiful day for a round a golf. Hermie had spent the whole night unable to sleep after his conversation with Cal. He was in eager anticipation of possibly finally getting used for a round of golf. His first round at least would be a tournament round.

That morning Donny came into the locker room to pick up the golf bag. The locker room attendant said, "How are you doing, Donny? Is Jack going to put together another good round?"

Donny said, "Sure hope so. We're in good position to win the tournament. Did you get the shoes cleaned and shined for me?"

"They're ready and over there." he told him.

"Thanks." said Donny. He then got the bag and shoes and me Jack, who was waiting outside by the pro shop. It wouldn't be long before they would be out on the course.

Hermie could hear the golfers talking about the course. He heard that the pins would be tucked away in corners on the greens. That would make low scoring very difficult today.

Hermie could hear Jack talking to Donny. He told him, "I've got the range balls. Lets go over to the range and get limbered up."

"Be right behind you." Donny answered.

It seemed this day would start the same as yesterday. Jack spent forty-five minutes on the range working on a variety of shots. He finished hitting the last five balls with his one wood.

Jack then said, "Let's go over to the putting green. Throw me three balls to putt with Donny."

Donny flipped Jack three balls. One of them was Hermie. On the putting green jack practiced putts from various distances. It seemed to Hermie he followed about the same routine on the green as yesterday. After about fifteen minutes, Jack threw the three balls back to Donny. He put them back into the bag.

Jack and Donny then walked over to the first tee to begin their round of golf. At the tee Jack greeted the starter, the other players and their caddies. Would this be the day that Hermie would finally get used in round of golf? Jack would be playing with the same two players he played with yesterday. They would be teeing off in the same order as well.

The first hole at the Ambassador Country Club was a straight par four with trees on both sides. Usually the first hole dictates what a course will be like. It is untrue here at this course.

The starter announced, "This is the eight forty tee time. On the tee is John Taggert from Topeka, Kansas. Will you please tee off."

"I'm using an Armor four ball." he told George and Jack. Then after a few practice swings, he launched the ball with what seemed to be a perfect swing. The ball flew into the air but veered to the right into the trees. Depending on where it finished, it could make par difficult to achieve.

"Next on the tee is Jack Hammer from Miami, Florida. Will you please tee off?" the starter announced.

Jack had Donny pull a ball and tee from the bag. It was Hermie. His big day had arrived. Hermie would find out what it was like to be a real golf ball. His two dreams of being used by a professional and playing in a tournament were coming true. Little did Hermie know he was about to begin one of the most memorable adventures of any golf ball.

Jack told the other players, "I'll be using an Excel one today. Good luck and play well." Donny handed Jack his one wood for he tee shot. Jack took a few warm-up swings before addressing the ball. Hermie closed his eyes and braced himself for the impact of the club. Soon, he would be flying through the air. Jack started his swing and had perfect timing. He impacted Hermie perfectly. "Ouch!!" bellowed Hermie flying through the air.

At first it hurt with the impact of the club but Hermie flew straight and true. He landed about two hundred and seventy yards from the tee right in the middle of the fairway. He rolled an additional twenty yards before he settled into the grass. Hermie promised himself next time he would keep his eyes open during the flight.

"The final player in the group is George Pullmer from Los Angeles, California. Please tee off." announced the starter.

"I'll be using a Pilot two." George told the other players. With a few practice swings his tee shot flew into the air. His ball finished in the middle of the fairway just ten yards behind where Hermie was.

Lying in the middle of the fairway Hermie began to daydream. He thought about the upcoming adventures that he might be in store for. He wondered and hoped that he wouldn't get lost or end up in a water hazard. He looked around and a little behind him was another golf ball. It was the Pilot ball that George was using. In a soft voice Hermie said, "Hi. My name is Hermie. What's yours?"

"My name is Mike. I see you are one of those new Excel balls. I'm a Pilot ball. Hope we have a good round. Maybe we can talk more later."

Soon Mike was flying through the air towards the green. Jack and Donny then arrived where Hermie was laying in the fairway. Jack said to Donny, "Slight breeze coming from the left and about how far do you think?"

Donny told him, "There's a ridge right behind where the pin is and it's about one hundred ten yards to it. Looks like an easy pitching wedge to me."

Donny handed Jack the pitching wedge and he prepared for the next shot. He struck it with confidence he had on his tee shot. Hermie didn't feel the pain this time. He flew through the air and landed softly on the green. He backed up only slightly and finished some three feet from the pin. It would be an excellent chance for a birdie and a great way to begin the round.

John had hit a remarkable shot from the trees onto the green. George had hit the green as well. Hermie was closest. When all three players arrived at the green, they marked their balls with coins. Hermie would now get to feel what it was like to be cleaned by a towel. It tickled his cover. After George and John had putted and missed, it was Jacks' turn to putt. He lined up Hermie from all four sides. Then with the confidence he had showed on the practice putting green, he stroked Hermie right into the cup. It was a birdie for Jack and a great start. George and John both made their pars.

The second hole at the Ambassador Country Club is a long demanding par five hole. It is the hardest and number one handicap hole on the course. It is tree-lined on both sides and has water in front of the green. It would demand two accurate and solid shots to get home in two.

John said, "Nice birdie on the first hole, Jack. It's a great way to start your round. It's your honors."

Jack said, "Okay." He placed Hermie on a wooden tee. A few practice swings, exact timing and Hermie flew straight and true. With his eyes open Hermie could see over the whole course and how big it was. Hermie landed in the dead center of the fairway about two hundred and seventy yards off the tee. He then rolled about another thirty yards.

George and John hit their tee shots in the middle of the fairway as well. They didn't up as far as Hermie. The three players would have to make a decision whether to go for the green in two or lay up.

George would be hitting first with the shortest of the

three drives. He decided to go for the green in two. He launched his shot. He ball landed right in the center of the water hazard. Mike was lost.

John would be next to hit. It's always hard to hit after a fellow competitor has just hit into the water. John decided to go for the green in two as well. Trying to avoid the water he pulled his shot left into the trees and out of bounds. After that he decided with his provisional ball to lay up short of the water.

Jack was now up. He turned to Donny and said, "Well, we saw what they did. Do you think we should still go for the green?"

Donny answered, "I feel with a solid shot we can do it with no problem. We planned our strategy before the round started. Going for the green in two was what we intended to do. It's about two hundred and forty yards to carry the water. Here's your three wood."

Donny had confidence in Jack. Hermie was unsure and nervous. His fibers tingled and perspiration dripped over his dimples. He had seen the Pilot ball he had just me plop into the water. The other ball he never got to talk to was lost in the woods. Two nervous occurrences for any golf ball to witness.

Jack agreed with Donny. He was going for the green in two. Hermie swallowed hard. The water and the woods is where no golf ball wants to be. Hermie braced himself for what may lie ahead. With a few extra practice swings and a deep breath Jack executed what seemed to be a perfect timed swing. He impacted Hermie solidly and he flew straight as an arrow. Hermie flew completely over the water to his relief and landed on the green. He rolled only a little before finishing some thirty-five feet from the pin. Hermie was relieved and proudly waited for Jack to arrive.

George and John both hit pitch shots onto the green after their wayward shots. John was laying five and had a ten-foot putt for bogey. George was laying four and had a ten-foot putt remaining for par.

George said to Jack, "Great second shot. You really must have caught it solid."

John said, "Good shot, Jack."

Jack said, "Thanks." He tipped his cap to the applause of the small crowd watching. He then marked Hermie with a coin and gave him a slight smooch. Donny cleaned Hermie off with a towel and tossed him back to Jack. Jack remarked him on the green and started figuring out the line for his putt. He studied it carefully from all four sides.

He then whispered to Donny, "I think it will break to the right at the end about a foot. What do you think?"

Donny told him, "I agree. Remember the grain of the grass is against you so the putt will be slower."

With those factors taken into consideration Jack prepared for this important putt. A deep breath to relax and few extra practice strokes Hermie was rolling on his way towards the hole. He took the break just as Jack had figured. The only question was did he hit it hard enough. Hermie got to the hole and rested on the lip and then dropped into the cup.

Donny raised his hands and shouted, "EAGLE!!"

Jack was much calmer for all he did was raise his putter into the air and acknowledge the applause from the crowd.

STEPHEN R. MUELLER

He realized there was a lot more golf yet to be played. Jack pulled Hermie from the cup and gave him a big kiss. Hermie was embarrassed. It was a great start to a round of golf. Hermie also knew that there were many more hazards coming up.

As Jack had success on the hole, George and John both suffered double bogies. George three putted from ten feet while John two putted. There was much work ahead for both of them to get back into contention.

Jack and Donny walked at a quick pace over to the third tee. The others followed behind pondering what had just occurred on the last hole. The third through the seventh holes provided no additional excitement for any of the players. All three players made routine uneventful pars on every hole. Jack continued to use Hermie while the other players changed their balls frequently. So through the first seven holes Jack was three under par and George and John were both two over. It wasn't until the short par three eighth hole that things heated up again.

The eighth hole at the Ambassador Country Club was a short but tricky par three. The green sat on a knoll with a large sand trap in front, two small traps on the left side and a deep slope in back. There was a small pond in front of the tee with a fountain in it. It mainly was for show and to scare the members of they topped their tee shot. It demanded an accurate and exact shot. When the wind blew, the hole was one of the more difficult on the course.

Jack asked Donny, "Well, what club do you think?"

Donny told him, "The pin is tucked fifteen feet behind

the sand trap that means the ball needs to carry at one hundred and sixty yards. I would choose a seven iron."

Jack said, "Alright, lets use a seven iron."

Hermie felt Jack and Donny together made a good team. He was confident the club selected would be right. Jack addressed the ball, a few practice swings and made what seemed a perfect swing. Hermie flew straight towards the pin but a gust of wind caught him. He plugged into the sand trap guarding the front of the green. He was buried in the sand. This was a new experience for Hermie. The sand felt cool around his cover. He also wondered how hard it would be for Jack to get him out. George and John negotiated the hole better than Jack. They finished with short putts for birdies on the green.

When Jack arrived where Hermie was laying in the trap, he had a disappointed look noticing Hermie was buried. He told Donny, "It looks like I got more than I bargained for. I'll need to play an explosion shot. Let me have my sand wedge."

Donny handed him the club and picked up the rake that was laying nearby. Hermie had gained confidence in Jack over the round. He was still nervous and there was tingling in his fibers about the shot he faced. Hermie wished he could yell out and tell Jack you can do it.

Jack prepared to explode Hermie from the sand. Jack shifted his shoes back and forth into the sand to make sure of firm footing. By the rules of golf, Jack couldn't let the club touch the sand at address. Jack made a steep upright swing. The sand exploded and Hermie popped out of the sand right onto the green. The over spin from the buried lie in the trap made Hermie roll on the green like a putt. He went straight towards the cup and dropped in. Donny jumped for glee and the audience clapped wildly. Jack raised his club into the air and acknowledged the accolades by tipping his cap. Jack and Donny tried to control their emotions. They knew that this was a tournament and there were many more holes left to play.

Jack climbed out of the trap to congratulations from all three caddies, the gallery and his fellow competitors. Jack went over to the cup and pulled Hermie out. He gave him a large smooch on the cover as if saying thank you. Both George and John made their birdie putts so it was a great hole for the entire group.

As they arrived at the ninth tee, Hermie had a special tingle inside. He couldn't realize how close he was to his good friend, Bernie. Jack would be teeing off first after his miraculous birdie on the previous hole. He put Hermie on a wooden tee. With a few practice swings and a well-timed swing Hermie flew straight and true unlike Bernie had. Hermie ended up in the middle of the fairway with only a short approach to the green. Both George and John hit their tee shots in the middle as well.

With the other balls close by, Hermie took advantage to get to know them. He said, "Hi. My name is Hermie. It's been pretty exciting golf so far."

"Hi. My name is Randy. I'm a Pilot ball. I see you're an Excel ball. Have you been used before in a tournament."

"No. This is my first experience on a golf course. I'm sorry your friend Mike got lost in the water." Hermie answered.

"I was used once before in a tournament." the other golf ball said, whose name was Barry. "I got lost once but only for a short while. The caddie found me under some leaves luckily."

"Weren't you worried?" inquired Hermie.

"At first but then I heard footsteps and relaxed." said Barry.

"I sure hope I don't get lost in the woods. It's so lonely and scary." Hermie said. It happened to be ironic that he said this. Hermie couldn't realize that Bernie was less than twenty yards from where he was. If Bernie only had some way of letting Hermie know where he was.

Soon Jack got up to where Hermie was lying. Talking with Donny coming up the fairway Jack already knew what club he needed to use. Soon Hermie was flying through the air. He ended up some fifteen feet from the cup. George and John both hit their second shots on the green. Their shots finished inside of Hermie.

The three players arrived at the green to a nice applause from the gallery. They all marked their balls with coins and cleaned them off. Since Jack was the farthest away, he would be putting first. He lined up his putt from all four sides. There was a murmur in the gallery that if he made this putt he would shoot five under par for the front side. With a deep breath Jack stroked Hermie perfectly and accurately. Just like Hermie had eyes, he rolled right into the cup. Jack raised his fist and Donny jumped in elation. What a front side Jack had played and Hermie had played an intricate part. The applause was deafening as Jack pulled Hermie from the cup. He gave him even a bigger smooch this time. Jack put Hermie into his pocket.

George and John after the applause clamed down were both able to make their birdie putts as well. The group as a whole had played the last two holes in six under. George and John both had staged a nice comeback and finished even par.

The first nine was over and Jack had shot five under par. The three players would have about a twenty-minute break before they would start the second nine. The one question Hermie had was if Jack would continue using him. He would know in about twenty minutes.

CHAPTER 8
The Second Nine

There was a buzz in the clubhouse and gallery. Jack had just shot one of the best front nines in the long history of the tournament. The only question was if he could keep it going. Jack couldn't to anywhere without people wanting to shake his hand or pat him on the back. What he really needed was some quiet time before the next nine to relax and reflect.

Jack went inside the pro shop and told Al, "The course is in great condition. You should be really proud of your greenskeeping crew. I'm sure glad the wind isn't blowing hard though."

Al told him, "Thanks, Jack. Good luck the second nine. Talk to you when you're done."

Stopping in the pro shop and talking to Al gave Jack a few minutes to relax away from the crowds. It was something he needed. He met Donny outside the pro shop. He had bought Jack a hot dog and coke for nourishment before the second nine. The three players and their caddies then walked over to the tenth tee. The gallery swelled. Almost five thousand spectators lined the fairway. It would be a fun and exciting back nine.

Donny then asked Jack, "Do you want to change balls for the second nine?" Hermie was about to find out the answer to his one question.

Jack told him, "No. I don't want to change my luck." Hermie was relieved. Jack, Donny or Hermie could know what was in store for them. It could be amazing and unforgettable. It also could be a nightmare.

The tenth hole was a duplicate of the first hole. It was tree-lined from the tee to the green. The only difference was the six sand traps. Two guarded the fairway about two hundred fifty yards from the tee while the other four surrounded a small green. A straight tee shot and an accurate pitch could easily lead to a welcomed birdie.

Jack had the honors on the tenth tee. He told George and John, "I'll still be using the number one Excel ball." He pulled Hermie and a tee from his pocket. Then with a whisper to Hermie he said, "Lets see if we can do even better this nine." He then placed him on the tee. A few stretching exercises, a few practice swings and a deep breath an Hermie was launched into the air. He flew straight as an arrow landing in the dead center of the fairway. Jack would only have a short pitch to the green.

George and John didn't change balls either. Their tee shots found the middle of the fairway as well but not as far as Hermie had gone. The three balls would be able to talk to one another till the players arrived.

Barry asked Hermie, "What did Jack whisper to you?"

He told me, "Lets try and do even better this nine."

Randy chuckled and said, "If you do even better this nine, you should have no problem winning this tournament."

"Do you really think so?" Hermie said hopefully.

The players arrived just then. George hit first and his second shot missed the sand traps and found the green about ten feet from the cup. John hit his second shot a couple of feet inside that. Then came Jack who executed a perfect wedge shot inside both of them.

George sarcastically said, "Here we go again."

The applause was deafening as the three players reached the green. They repaired their ballmarks and marked their balls with coins. George, being the farthest away, would go first. George made a confident stroke and knocked the ball right into the cup. John followed suit with a solid putt right into the cup. Jack then replaced Hermie onto the green and what seemed rather quickly, rapped Hermie into the cup. The second nine was in high gear with all three players starting with birdies. There was a constant applause as the players left the green to the next tee.

Things calmed down the next three holes where all the players managed solid uneventful pars. The string of birdies was broken. Jack, after thirteen holes today, was six under par while George and John were both one under.

The fourteenth hole at the Ambassador County Club is a par four that's tree-lined on both sides. It has two fairway sand traps strategically placed about two hundred and seventy yards off the tee. It demands accuracy off the tee and confidence in your swing.

Jack would have the honors. He placed Hermie on a tee. Jack had decided to use his driver for he had confidence he could fly the traps. A smooth swing and Hermie was launched. Jack didn't feel he caught Hermie solid and he was right. Hermie landed just short of the traps and bounced in. He wasn't buried but it would be a challenge just to get to the green. George and John both laid up short of the traps but would have long second shots to a small green.

George and John had about two hundred yards left to green. They both hit excellent second shots and ended up in birdie range on the green. Meanwhile, Jack was standing next to Donny looking at the sand shot that faced him. Donny then said, "We have about one hundred and eighty yards to clear the trap in front and one hundred ninety total to get to the green."

"Alright. Let me have a four iron. I'll need a little loft to clear the lip of the trap." Jack executed what seemed to be a perfect swing. Hermie flew right out of the sand and landed on the green with such force that he made a deep divot and spun backwards. He finished only six feet from the cup.

"Great shot, Jack. I really didn't think you had enough club." said Donny.

"I hit that shot exactly the way I wanted to. It felt great and very satisfying. It's the kind of shot that makes you glad you play golf." said Jack.

As the three players walked towards the green, the gallery applauded their great second shots. George then said, "Now if we can just finish them off with some great putts." Both Jack and John acknowledged the applause as they stepped onto the green. They repaired their ballmarks and marked their balls. John would be putting first.

John then remarked his ball and prepared to putt. His putt had too much speed and rimmed to cup. He would have to settle for par. George suffered the same fate as John. His putt also rimmed out causing him to settle for par as well. Jack was up. He replaced Hermie where the coin was and started to line up the putt. He consulted with Donny, "So, what do you thing?"

Donny said, "You saw how the other balls broke sharply at the cup, so watch your speed and just knock the ball into the cup." With that, Jack confidently made two practice strokes, played a little less break and rapped Hermie firmly right into the back of the cup. It was another birdie for Jack. According to the scoreboard next to the green Jack was now leading the tournament. Knowing that, made Hermie bubble with excitement. He only wished that his friend Bernie could share the excitement with him.

Speaking of Bernie, he still remained unfound in the woods off the ninth fairway. People during the day could be heard rumbling through the woods but no one seemed to look where Bernie was. He wondered how much longer he would have to spend amongst the trees and the squirrels. He often wondered and thought about his friend Hermie. He really missed him.

The fifteenth hole at the Ambassador Country Club is the last par three on the course. With the green completely surrounded by water it demands an accurate high shot to hold the green. The hole plays extremely difficult when it is windy.

Jack had the honors after his birdie on the last hole. He looked over to Donny, put a hand on his shoulder and asked him, "Well, what do you thin?"

Donny told him, "They put the pin fifteen feet onto the green. I figure you need to carry about one hundred and sixty yards."

Jack told him, "With the little wind there is, I figure a solid seven iron should do the trick. We used that club during the first found. Wind is blowing about the same."

"Sounds good to me." Donny confirmed.

Jack placed Hermie on a wooden tee. Hermie was nervous about flying over the water. He remembered back on the front nine when that one ball he had just talked to went into the water. Hermie would just have to brace himself and pray Jack hits a solid shot. Jack did just that as Hermie flew straight as an arrow over the water straight towards the green. He landed about six feet behind the hole. With a slight divot he spun back. The contour of the green caused Hermie to roll just like a putt and right back in to cup.

Donny yelled, "It's a HOLE-IN-ONE!!!!!!"

The applause was deafening and could be heard all over the course. Jack raised his club and tipped his cap in acknowledgement. Both George and John shook his hand and even hugged him. John then said, "I sure hope some of your luck rubs off on us." With that said and a calming in the applause George and John both managed to hit their shots onto the green.

The entire time they were walking down to the green, the applause was constant and deafening. When the group arrived at the green, Jack pulled Hermie out of the cup, hoisted him into the air and the applause erupted again. He then gave Hermie a big kiss of thanks. Hermie seemed to blush from all the attention. Jack then tucked Hermie safely away in his pocket. It made Hermie wonder if he would be used again.

George and John both were able to negotiate their short birdie putts. It had been a perfect hole for all three of them. The crowd was in a buzz as they walked over to the next tee. There was a whispering in the crowd that Jack was nine under par for the day. The competitive course record of sixty-two, which was established about ten years ago by Jim Jackson, could be in jeopardy of being broken. People have always said records are made to be broken.

On the way over to the tee Donny asked, "Jack, do you want to use a different ball?"

Hermie took a big gulp. Jack said, "No, Donny. I don't want to change anything right now." Hermie was relieved and wanted to give Jack a big smooch.

The players sat on the bench waiting for the green ahead to clear. The sixteenth hole at the Ambassador Country Club is a unique hole. It's a short par four over water that can be driven if the player is willing to take the gamble. An accurate shot can reward you, while an errant shot can penalize you severely. There was a safety area provided where players could take the safer route and have a short pitch left to the green. Each player needed to decide if the gamble was worth it.

Waiting on the tee the players talked among themselves. Hermie and the other balls were on the ground in front. Hermie whispered to one of the other balls, "Did you hear that I almost got replaced?"

STEPHEN R. MUELLER

Barry told him, "If I would of just made a hole-in-one, I would have been put in his pocket immediately afterwards and never used again. You're lucky to still be used by Jack. He really feels you bring him luck." Hermie wanted to talk more but the players were getting ready to tee off.

Jack turned to Donny with a smile on his face, "Well, I had no problem clearing the water during my practice round or first round. Lets go for it. Let me have the one wood." The gallery erupted again in applause, for jack was taking the gamble of going for the green. The question was answered about taking the conservative route.

Jack placed Hermie on a wooden tee. He took a deep breath, determined the direction of the flight of the ball he desired and took a few extra practice swings. With a final swing of the club Hermie was airborne and flying over the water. Jack had caught Hermie solid but could he hold the green. Hermie impacted the green with great force that caused a large divot. He then bounced several times before finishing in the sand trap behind the green. He had cleared the water and was safe.

Donny turned to Jack, "Great shot!!" The gallery applauded loudly in appreciation of Jack going for the green. George and John acknowledged the great tee shot as well. George and John took the safe route and would have only short pitches left to the green.

Briskly the players walked to where their tee shots had finished. The gallery followed them in eager anticipation of what may happen next. George and John got up to their balls first. Both of them negotiated accurate pitch shots and would have short birdie putts left.

Jack prepared for his sand shot. He stepped down into the sand and pondered the shot that faced him. Hermie wasn't buried but instead was on the upslope of the trap. This made the shot less difficult but the situation made it a little harder. Donny handed Jack his sand wedge. He dug his shoes into the sand and with an upright swing Hermie exploded out of the sand. Hermie took one bounce and dropped right into the cup. Jack put his head between his knees. He couldn't believe what was happening. It was every golfers dream to have a round like this. The gallery went into an enthusiastic applause. It could be heard over the whole golf course.

Jack stepped out of the trap onto the green with the gallery still applauding. He walked over to the hole and pulled Hermie out and gave him a big smooch. Jack had made an eagle and was now eleven under par for his round today. Jack and his playing partners couldn't recall a round of golf like this in their many years of playing.

There was still a hum in the crowd. After the applause subsided, George and John were able to safely negotiate their putts for birdies on the hole. The group as a whole was four under for this particular hole. The gallery was growing even larger as the players moved towards the seventeenth tee. Everyone was in eager anticipation of what my happen next.

The seventeenth hole was a narrow long dogleg tree-lined par four. It had three sand traps guarding the fairway and three traps guarding the green. One of the traps on the right side of the fairway was the biggest on the course. It often slowed play because of the problems players had. It gave the players behind a chance to relax and think.

Sitting on the bench the players talked about what had occurred on the previous hole. Hermie on the ground in front of them could hear what they said. Jack spoke, "The last hole sure provided some special excitement for the gallery. Did you get an opportunity to look over at the scoreboard? It looks like there are a lot of good rounds being shot today."

George asked, "Are you still using the new Excel ball? You must really like it. I was thinking about changing to it as well."

Jack told him, "It performs great and I plan to keep on using it." A real big smile came over Hermie. He was really proud to be an Excel ball. At the same time it made him think of his friend Bernie. He wondered where he was.

Hermie looked over at one of the other balls, "Did you hear that?"

"Looks like you got job security." the other ball told him with a snicker and a chuckle.

The players were getting ready to tee off. All three players managed to hit their tee shots in the middle of the fairway. While Hermie waited, he reminisced about the fun conversation he would have with Bernie if he ever saw him again. He really missed him. All three players luckily had avoided the large fairway sand trap. With the shortest drive, Jack would be hitting his second shot first. He seemed to take a little more time selecting a club and preparing for the shot. After a deep breath and a few extra practice swings, Jack launched Hermie into the air. He flew straight as an arrow towards the green. He landed on the green, rolled very little but finished a long way from the cup. Jack would have about a fifty-foot putt for birdie. It was one of the least accurate shots Jack had hit all day. Nerves were probably playing a significant part in this.

George and John hit their second shots inside of where Hermie was laying. Jack would be putting first. When Jack arrived at the green, he marked Hermie with a coin and had Donny clean him off. Jack told Donny, "Looks like we got a long birdie putt. Have any ideas about the break and grain?"

Donny told him, "The grain will be against you the whole putt and it breaks sharply to the left right near the cup. Just use the same touch and stroke you've been using and you'll do great."

Jack told him, "Thanks, I'll keep that in mind."

Jack remarked Hermie. He surveyed the putt from all four sides and took into consideration what Donny had told him. He decided to have Donny tend the pin. With a few deliberate practice strokes Hermie was soon rolling across the green. He veered to the left more than Jack had allowed and stopped some five feet away.

Jack remarked Hermie and would wait his turn to finish up. George and John both made wonderful putts for birdies. Jack would now need to negotiate the final five feet for his par. He placed Hermie in front of the coin and rather quickly prepared to putt. Nerves were definitely playing a part. A few quick practice strokes and Hermie rolled firmly into the back of the cup. He made his par and now there was only one more hole to go.

When the players got to the eighteenth tee, the gallery had swelled to an enormous size. You could feel the excitement in the air and the pressure building. Everyone in the gallery knew what the situation was. Jack, with a par, would establish a new competitive course record. He would also have what you could say was an insurmountable lead of ten strokes.

The finishing hole here at the club was a challenging, long narrow par five hole with disaster written all over it. The fairway had numerous undulations causing treacherous stances and lies. Along with the trees guarding both sides a large lake guarded the left side of the fairway all the way to the green. Two large sand traps guarded the other side of the fairway. Two other sand traps guarded the green as well. The hold demanded two accurate and solid shots to get home in two. Then when you got to the green the real fun began. The green is the largest on the course. Most putts will have two breaks and many will have mounds and valleys to negotiate. It isn't unusual to have putts of over one hundred feet to the hole.

George would tee off first. He launched his tee shot. It veered to the right and finished on the edge of the rough. John hit his tee shot to the right as well but it finished in the fairway sand trap. Jack was now up. Jack, still using Hermie, placed him on a tee. Hermie fell off the tee. Jack reteed Hermie, took a few extra practice swings and with a deep breath launched Hermie off the tee. Hermie, unlike the other balls, landed in the dead center of the fairway but hit one of the mounds. He rolled only a little further before stopping and leaving a severe uphill lie for the next shot. Hermie really wished Bernie could be experiencing what was going on in this tournament.

George would be hitting his second shot first. He decided to not go for the green and laid up in position for an easy pitch. John had a long fairway bunker shot. The lip of the trap forced John to use a sand wedge just to get the ball out. He would be facing a long third shot.

Jack turned to Donny, "What do you think?"

Donny told him, "You have about two hundred and fifty yards to the green. You also have about one hundred and eighty yards to the lay up area. A good three wood shot because of the severity of the uphill lie might put you on the front of the green. You would then be facing a very long treacherous putt."

Jack told him, "We haven't played conservative all day. Let me have the three wood."

Jack stood there a minute trying to visualize the shot. He took a few practice swings and a deep breath. With a confident swing he launched Hermie into the air. Hermie flew over the water and landed just on the front edge of the green. The crowd erupted into applause in appreciation of the gamble Jack had taken. He would have a putt in excess of one hundred feet but at least he was on the green and dry. Jack acknowledged the applause by tipping his cap. Jack also got a high-five and handshake from Donny. They both walked together acknowledging the applause as they went.

John was able to negotiate his long third shot. It finished some sixty feet from the cup. George was able to hit his pitch within ten feet of the cup. He would have a level putt for his birdie. As the three players and their caddies arrived near the green, the gallery gave them a rousing ovation. Everyone appreciated the great golf the three players had played.

Jack marked Hermie first and tossed him to Donny. He whispered, "Clean him well, Donny."

Donny tossed Hermie back to Jack. Jack placed Hermie back down in place of the coin and began the task of lining him up. There was a hush in the crowd. You could of heard a pin drop. Hermie, sitting on the green alone, got a chance to look around. There were people everywhere. All the eyes seemed like they were staring at him and they were. Hermie seemed to perspire. Jack conferred with Donny, "It looks like a roller coaster not a putt."

Donny told him, "The putt will be slow because the grain is mostly against you. The mound about halfway will cause the putt to break a little more to the right. Just put a confident solid stroke on the ball and trust yourself."

Hermie wished he could tell Jack how much he believed in him. A complete quiet was over the whole gallery. Jack addressed the ball. Hermie could see the sweat rolling down off his face. A few practice strokes and two deep breathes and Hermie was on his way. With Donny tending the pin Hermie rolled across the green. He rolled a little to the left and then to the right. He then straightened out right towards the cup. Hermie kept on rolling for what seemed an eternity. He approached the cup and stopped right on the lip. A few seconds went by. PLOP!!! into the cup Hermie fell. Jack threw his putter into the air and dropped to his knees. It had been an emotional draining round of golf for Jack. He got up to his feet to the greeting of a big hug from Donny and a huge applause from the gallery. Jack tipped his cap and walked towards the cup. He picked Hermie out of the cup, kissed him and held him high into the air.

Jack raised his hands into the air to ask for quiet so George and John could finish putting as well. Both of them two putted for pars. All three players received a standing ovation as they left the green towards the scorers' tent. Hermie all this time was safely in Jacks' front pocket.

In the scorers' tent the three players got a drink of water and sat down to verify their scorecards. George told Jack, "It will be a privilege and an honor to sign and verify your score."

Jack told both George and John, "It was an honor to play the first two rounds with you both. Good luck the rest of the tournament. Maybe when the tourney is over we can have a beer or two together."

With that said they signed their respective scorecards. The man in the tent said, "It would be a honor to shake the hand of someone who has just shot a fifty-nine. Jack obliged him and smiled. All three players then left the scorers' tent.

CHAPTER 9
The Tournament Ends

The memorable second round was over. Jack had spent hours in the news tent answering a wide variety of questions. All that time Hermie was tucked away in his pocket. When the news conference was over, Jack and Donny spent another two hours practicing on the range and putting. It was dark when they left the course.

Two rounds of the tournament were over. Jack led by ten strokes with a score of seventeen under par. With the brilliant second round Jack had played, he had established five new tournament records. It could be a restless night at the hotel wondering what tomorrow might bring.

Surprisedly, Hermie had remained in the pocket of Jack instead of the golf bag. Jack kept Hermie with him when he went to the hotel, out to eat and even put him in the ashtray before going to sleep. Hermie was all-alone with nobody to talk to. Hermie began to wonder if he would ever be used again or what would happen. Would he end up in the shag bag now? Would he see any of his friends again especially Bernie? He wondered why he was in the hotel room. A strange place for a golf ball he thought.

That night in the hotel, while Jack snored noisily, Hermie had a restless night. The morning light couldn't come quickly enough for him. Jack woke up when his alarm went off and took a big stretch. He took a shower, shaved and got ready for the round today. He put Hermie back in his pocket again all alone. Hermie wondered what might be in store.

Jack stopped and picked up Donny at his home where they went to a restaurant to get something to eat. Off to the course after eating they went with Hermie tucked away safely with Jack in his pocket. At the course, the parking attendant directed Jack to the designated parking area set aside for players. There Jack met Simon, one of the fellow competitors. Jack and Simon had played together in the last tournament. Simon told Jack, "That was a great round you had yesterday. They'll talk about that for quite a while." "Thanks, Simon. You hit them well today." Jack told him. With their shoes and gear, they shook hands and walked towards the clubhouse. Both players went into the pro shop to register. Donny waited outside with the other caddies.

Inside the pro shop they checked their tee times and whom they would be playing the next round with. The tee times are determined by your position in the tournament. Jack would be in the final group to go off. Jack would be playing with two players who had beaten him before recently. Hermie, meanwhile, remained all this time close to

Jack in his pocket. Jack said, "Hi, Al. I need three new Excel balls and range balls."

Al told him, "You have a round like you did yesterday and no one will catch you this tournament. By the way did you try that Excel ball?

Jack told him "I used one the whole round. They're great."

Al then told him, "Good luck and hit them straight."

Jack told Donny outside, "Put this ball, which was Hermie, in the front compartment of the golf bag. It was the special ball we used yesterday and I want it close to bring good luck. Put the other Excel balls in the regular place."

Jack and Donny walked over to the range. They practiced for about forty-five minutes and walked over to the putting green. Donny asked Jack, "Do you want to use that same Excel ball or the new ones?"

Jack told Donny, "No, that ball is only for special occasions. I'll use one of the three new Excel balls I just bought for the round today."

Jack putted for about twenty minutes when the starter announced the ten o'clock tee time. It was time for Jack to play his third round. Hermie was in the golf bag where everything was quiet. All he could do was wonder what was happening. He had no one to talk to.

The third round went nothing like the second round. It was definitely more typical golf. It concluded with Hermie never being used and Jack still leading the tournament after shooting a steady round of sixty-eight. Verifying his scorecard and spending almost two hours in the press tent answering questions. Jack went to his golf bag and pulled out

Hermie. He gave him a smooch and put him in his pocket. Jack and Donny spent the next two hours on the range and left the course when it was dark.

Hermie was thankful to Jack for having used him in the second round but wanted to tell him how boring it was in a pocket all by yourself. That night Hermie ended up in the ashtray at the hotel just like yesterday. It would be another boring and long night for him.

During the night all Hermie could think about was what the upcoming day might bring. Would he be all alone or have someone new to talk to? He also wondered where his good friend Bernie might be. Hermie wondered if Bernie was as bored as he was.

The next morning Jack got ready for the fourth and final round. He showered, shaved, got dressed and put Hermie in his pocket. There was a sense of urgency and nervousness about. When Jack was ready, he left the hotel, and went to pick up Donny. They stopped an ate some breakfast, then off to the course.

A parking attendant directed them to where go park. The gallery was enormous in size. People were parked everywhere. People were even waiting around the special lot to possibly get autographs from some of the players.

Jack put on his golf shoes while Donny got the golf bag ready. They both then walked to the pro shop. Jack went inside while Donny waited outside. Al greeted him, "Good Morning, Jack. What can I help you with?"

"I need to check my tee time and pick up some range balls." Jack answered.

Al handed Jack a basket of range balls and told him his tee

time. He said, "Have a good round today and I'll see you when you are finished."

"Thanks, Al for all your hospitality." said Jack. He then met Donny outside. Together they walked over to the practice range where they spent forty-five minutes limbering up and practicing a variety of shots. Meanwhile, all this time Hermie remained in his pocket. Hermie wondered could this final round be the special occasion Jack referred to for him to be used again.

Jack finished practicing on the range and left for the putting green. Donny pulled two balls from the golf bag while Jack pulled Hermie from out of his pocket. Finally, some action Hermie thought. Was the special occasion that Jack was referring to the fourth round of the tournament? It was nice to feel the green grass against his cover though it was only the putting green. Twenty minutes went by and the starter announced their tee time. Donny put all the balls in the golf bag including Hermie.

They walked over to the first tee to start the fourth and final round. Jack shook the hands of his fellow competitors, the starter and the caddies. Soon Hermie would know whether or not he was going to be used for this final round.

Jack would be teeing off last because he was the leader of the tournament. Jack reached into his golf bag. Instead of Hermie, he pulled out a friend of his, Jeremy. He was the lucky choice for this important final round. The only satisfaction to Hermie was that jack was using one of his friends and an Excel ball as well.

Over the next five hours, which seemed like an eternity, Hermie remained unused in the golf bag. At least he had someone to visit with, not like yesterday. In the pocket, where Hermie was, there was a scorecard showing the score of the second round. It made Hermie proud of all the eagles and birdies. He was especially proud of the fifty-nine.

In the golf bag Hermie could hear the applause of the gallery. Sometimes he heard Jack and Donny talk. Finally, Donny unzipped the pocket and dropped Jeremy and some tees inside. Hermie asked Jeremy, "Is the round over or is Jack changing balls?"

Jeremy told him, "The round was over and Jack played great. He won the tournament by ten strokes. It was great to be part of it." Telling this to Hermie brought a smile to his face. Now, he wondered what would be up next.

Hermie soon found out. Jack unzipped the golf pocket where Hermie was and put him in his pants pocket. Hermie thought to himself was this his destiny to end in a players pocket as a good luck charm. He would have no one to talk to. There would also be no way of ever seeing Bernie again.

The tournament was over and Jack was the champion. An award ceremony would be held on the eighteenth green. John Abraham, president of the Ambassador Country Club, would preside over the ceremonies. Present would be Jack, Peter Torkle, the runner-up, Al, Harvey and other dignitaries.

Mr. Abraham addressed the crowd, "First I wish to thank all of you who attended our tournament. It provided us with lots of excitement and unbelievable shotmaking. We hope you enjoyed it. Next I would like to say congratulations to Jack Hammer for winning the tournament in record fashion. He provided us with neverending excitement and magnificent shotmaking. I would like to now present Jack Hammer with the trophy and winners' check of this years tournament."

Jack approached the microphone. Mr. Abraham shook his hand. He handed him the trophy and the winners' check. The photographers took their pictures for the newspapers and magazines. Jack then addressed the crowd.

Jack said, "First, I would like to thank Mr. Abraham and the staff here at the Ambassador Country Club for hosting a class A event. I look forward to coming back next year and defend my title. I would also like to thank a couple of special people. First, my caddie Donny, who did a great job throughout the tournament. Secondly, I would to thank Mr. Al Hart and his staff. The golf course was in excellent condition. Finally, I would like to thank the gallery for coming out to watch us play. See you again next year."

With that said jack received a loud applause. The tournament was over and Hermie remained in his pocket throughout the ordeal. Hermie was proud of what Jack had accomplished and that he was able to play a small part in it. He only wished that Bernie was there to enjoy it with him.

CHAPTER 10
The Display Case

When the award ceremony was over, Mr. Abraham tapped Jack on the shoulder. Mr. Abraham asked him, "Could you please come to my office to discuss some private business. It will only take a few minutes."

Jack went with Mr. Abraham to his office. His office was decorated with classic golf pictures on all the walls. It was a gorgeous office. They sat down in some plush armchairs. Mr. Abraham the explained, "I would like the club to recognize your great accomplishments on the golf course. Your record winning tournament score and your fifty-nine in the second round deserve special recognition. What I would like to propose to the Board of Directors is that we have a display case in the center of the clubhouse rotunda.

In the display case there would be a plaque, a copy of your scorecard and the two golf balls you used during the tournament. One from the round of fifty-nine and one from the last eighteen would be nice. A replica of your trophy would also be displayed.

Jack said, with proudness in his voice, "That would be an honor and a privilege. When would you like them?"

Mr. Abraham asked, "How much longer will you be in town?"

Jack replied, "I'm taking off next week from the circuit. I'll be here another two or three days."

Mr. Abraham answered, "I'll call you at your hotel when we can meet and when the award ceremony will take place."

The next morning Jack got the phone call from Mr. Abraham. He told him to meet him at the club around one o'clock and to bring the golf balls for the display with him. Jack agreed.

When it was one o'clock, Jack met with Mr. Abraham in his office. Harvey Jacobs was there as well. Jack gave the two golf balls he had used to Mr. Abraham. Jack explained, "This one was used when I shot fifty-nine. The other was used in the last round." Hermie felt deserted when Jack handed him over. Mr. Abraham then gave them to Mr. Jacobs. He told Jack, "They will go great in the display case we have planned. Thank you."

Mr. Abraham then told Jack, "This display will show a duplicate scorecard, the two golf balls, the trophy and a plaque describing the accomplishment. Mr. Jacobs will take custody of the items until the display case is built. We will notify you when the ceremony will take place. It will probably take a few months for the case to be built."

Jack answered, "If my schedule allows me to, I will certainly be here. Thank you for this honor."

Hermie realized now that he would never be used on a golf course again. The only person he would be able to talk to was Jeremy. This made Hermie very sad. He realized his chances of ever seeing or finding Bernie again were extremely slim. Hermie had tears coming from his eyes.

Harvey put Hermie, Jeremy and the other items on a shelf in the closet of the pro shop. It was ironic for this was where Hermie and Jeremy had started their golfing lives at the Ambassador Country Club. They were back inside the closet where all the golfing supplies were stored. Hermie wondered.

Hermie let out a timid, "Hello."

There was silence at first but then a range ball spoke out, "Hey, it's Hermie and Jeremy. I thought you were bought and gone forever."

"No." said Hermie. "A touring professional bought me. I was used in the recent tournament along with Jeremy. We're going be displayed in a cabinet in the clubhouse rotunda. It will show our accomplishments during the tournament."

"What accomplishments were those?" one of the range balls with a puzzled look asked.

Hermie explained, "I was used in a course record round of fifty-nine. Jeremy was used in the last round when the tournament was won. Is Harry or Arnold around?"

One of the balls answered, "Harry was lost in the woods on the range and hasn't been heard from since. It has been over a week since he has been missing. As for Arnold he's resting over there. He had a very long week with the tournament and regular members busy practicing. Do you want me to wake him?"

"No." Hermie said. "I'll talk to him when he wakes up."

Suddenly a stirring was heard on a near shelf. Arnold was waking up from his snooze. "How are you doing sleepy head!" said Hermie.

With sleep still in his eyes Arnold muttered, "Oh! Hi Hermie. What brings you back to the closet? Have you been demoted to a range ball? What happened to the professional that bought you during the last tournament? Where is your good friend, Bernie?"

Hermie interrupted him, "If you would calm down Arnold, I'll tell you what's going on." So Arnold got comfortable on the shelf and began to listen. Arnold wasn't the only one listening. There was quietness in the closet to listen to what Hermie had to say.

Hermie began his story. "I was bought the first day of the tournament by a professional named Jack. A local golfer had bought Bernie a day earlier. I haven't seen him since. In the tournament just held in the second round Jack shot a course record fifty-nine. He went on to win the tournament by ten strokes. My friend, Jeremy, was used in the final round. The club, because of the course record and record winning score, is going to have a display case in the clubhouse rotunda displaying the trophy, us golf balls, a scorecard and a plaque. That's why I'm back inside the closet. I'm waiting here till the display case is built."

Arnold told him, "Congratulation to both of you. I suppose now you realize you will never get used again. At least you didn't end up in a shag bag. This last tournament wore out all of us balls completely. I have never been hit so many times before. By the way I'll keep an eye out for your friend, Bernie."

"You're a good friend, Arnold. Thanks." Hermie said.

Hermie and the other golf balls traded stories for what seemed weeks. Finally, one day Harvey came into the closet and picked up Hermie, Jeremy and the other tournament memorabilia. Hermie said good-bye to Arnold and the other equipment in the closet. He knew this time he would not be coming back.

Harvey brought the memorabilia to the lobby in the clubhouse. There Mr. Abraham and Mr. Hart met him. He placed the stuff on a table next to a big window. Hermie and Jeremy began to look around. They noticed a large figure in the middle of the rotunda covered in a sheet. They figured this was the display case and their final resting place.

Jack, who was able to attend the ceremony, brought a smile to both Hermie and Jeremy. They both wished they could hug him. Jack came over to the table where he smiled and winked. It was almost as if he were saying good-bye and thanks.

Mr. Abraham then spoke, "Attention everyone. Lets get the festivities underway. Welcome members, Mr. Hammer, Board of Directors, and distinguished guests. Not too long ago at our club we witnessed a great golfing accomplishment. The purpose of this festivity is to recognize it." Mr. Abraham went on, "Here at the Ambassador Country Club a professional tournament was held. One of the entrants was Jack Hammer. In the second round Mr. Hammer established a new course competitive course record by shooting a thirteen under par fifty-nine.

This bettered the old course record by three strokes. Jack went on to win the tournament with a record seventy-two hole scoring record as well. We at the Ambassador Country Club wish to recognize these accomplishments."

When Mr. Abraham was finished the sheet was removed that covered the display case. Standing in the middle of the rotunda was a magnificent breath-taking display. It was made of dark walnut and had glass panels on all four sides. There were small padded stands inside for the trophy and golf balls. It was gorgeous.

Jack then stepped up to the podium and said, "It's an honor to have my name and accomplishments associated with this beautiful display here at the Ambassador Country Club. I look forward to next year to defend my title, play even better and see this beautiful display case again. Thank you very much."

When Jack had finished talking, Mr. Abraham asked Harvey to bring over the items from the table that would be going into the cabinet. Mr. Abraham handed the items one at a time to Jack who put them inside the display where they belonged. This would probably be the last time that Jack would ever touch Hermie again. The case was then locked and everyone in attendance applauded.

Hermie was in his new home. Through the glass panes he could see the golf course, which brought a small smile to his face. He then turned to Jeremy and said, "I sure do wish that Bernie were here to enjoy this with me." With that said he cried.

Feeling sorry for Hermie, Jeremy said, "Did you notice that there was room in the display case for more trophies and balls? You never know what the future has in store."

CHAPTER 11
Found at Last

Little did Jeremy know how right he was with his thought. Another event was beginning to unfold. As the ceremony of the dedication in the clubhouse was ending, a young boy named Danny Wilson was searching for golf balls in the woods. It happened that this day he was looking on the ninth hole. Looking under twigs and leaves he spotted a dirty golf ball. It was Bernie.

Bernie had been lost in the woods for about three months. He had mud and stains all over him. Danny put Bernie into a bag he was holding. Bernie looked around at the other balls in the bag to see if he recognized anyone but he didn't. Danny kept on looking for balls for about another half hour before he headed for home. Bernie at least felt good that he had finally been found. Now he wondered where could his friend Hermie could be.

Danny rode his bike home from the course where he

brought the balls inside to clean them up. His father stopped him and asked, "Did you have any luck son?"

Danny told him, "I found about twenty golf balls. I'm going to take them to the basement and clean them. I want to use some of them in the upcoming tournament at the club." Danny went downstairs into the basement. He put the golf balls in a large sink and ran warm water. He used some soap and a sponge to get the grime off the balls. It felt very good to Bernie and the other balls.

Danny went upstairs to show his father the balls he had found after they were cleaned. His father inquired, "Where did you find most of them?"

Danny told him, "I found most of them in the woods on the ninth hole. I found only a few in the woods on the seventh hole."

His father then stated, "I see two of the balls you found are the new Excel balls. I suspect the professionals who played in the last tournament must of lost them."

Danny told his father proudly, "I plan to use one of them in the upcoming club championship." Danny was sixteen years old and the youngest to have ever qualified to play in the club championship. He had won a couple of other local events and played exceptionally well for his age. He had never faced the type of competition he would face in the club tournament though. He father was very proud of him and his accomplishments.

Hearing of the tournament perked up Bernie for then he could at least realize one of his dreams. Bernie also wondered what other Excel ball Danny had found. Did he know him? He looked around the other balls and saw the other Excel ball. It was Arturo.

"Hi. Arturo. It's me Bernie." he exclaimed.

"Howdy, Bernie. How did you end up in this unusual situation?" inquired Arturo.

Bernie told him, "After I was bought in the pro shop, I was used in a practice round before a tournament. On the ninth hole I ended up in the woods and was never found. The round was going really well until then. I spent many days among the squirrels, leaves and brush. Finally, I was found under some leaves. I overheard them talking about an upcoming tournament. Do you know what they could be talking about? Do you know what happened to my good friend Hermie? How did you end up here?"

Arturo told him, "I was bought a short time after you were and at the same time as your friend, Hermie. I was lost in the woods during a practice round for the tournament just played. That was the last time I saw Hermie or anyone else. I'm just glad someone found me and I have a chance to get on the course again."

Bernie then told him, "It was nice seeing you again. I look forward to getting on the course again. We'll talk some more later."

Danny told his father, "Goodnight. Remember tomorrow we're playing a practice round for the tournament this weekend."

"That reminds me, Danny. We received our tee times in the mail for the tourney. You tee off a half hour before I do. You will be playing with two older gentlemen, Max Blackburn and Mark Anderson. They have been members with the club quite a while and are good players. See you in the morning at seven. Goodnight, son." With that Danny hugged his father and went off to bed.

The next morning brought bright sunshine and a perfect day for a round of golf. Danny could smell the bacon cooking as he dressed faster than usual and hurried downstairs. His father was already at the table eating and told Danny, "Hurry up sleepy head, we don't want to miss our tee times."

Faster than usual Danny finished his breakfast, grabbed the golf clubs and was out to the car. About fifteen minutes later they were at the course. The course was quite crowded with all the players getting practice in before the tournament. Danny and his father went over to the pro shop to register. They had about twenty minutes until they teed off.

They both decided just to practice putting before they started. Danny was going to use one of his Excel balls he had found. He chose Arturo. Bernie was disappointed but hoped he would get to see Arturo again. For the rest of the day Bernie remained in the golf bag unused. Finally, after about five hours the zipper opened and Arturo, with some tees, dropped inside.

Arturo caught his breath. Bernie couldn't wait to talk to him. A few minutes later he asked, "How did the round go? At least it looks like this time you didn't get lost in the woods."

Arturo caught his breath and told him, "Danny played really well as did his father. He should do well in the upcoming tournament this weekend. I did hear him say he was going to use his other Excel ball tomorrow. That means you, Bernie."

Bernie was so excited he went, "Yippee!!"

The next few days would be very sleepless especially for Bernie. All he could do was think about being used again on a golf course. Best of all it was in a tournament. He couldn't wait for that day to come.

CHAPTER 12

The Comeback

It was Saturday and today was the club championship at the Ambassador Country Club. Danny woke up early to clean his shoes, clubs and balls. He put Bernie and a couple of other balls in his golf bag and went downstairs. There was his father already enjoying his breakfast.

"Well, Dad I'm ready to play." Danny excitedly blurted out.

His father told him, "First, eat your breakfast. Then we will go to the course."

Danny quickly ate his breakfast. He picked up the two golf bags and brought them out to the car. Soon his father came out and off to the course they went. There were quite a few cars in the parking lot when they arrived. Golfers were getting ready everywhere. You could feel a sense of tenseness in the air. Danny and his father put on their golf shoes, picked up their bags and off to the pro shop they went to register.

They walked through the clubhouse towards the pro shop. On the way they passed by a gorgeous wooden and glass display case. They stopped to admire it. Danny admired the accomplishments of Mr. Hammer. He also saw the stand that the club champion trophy would be on. It made Danny daydream and think. If Bernie only knew how close he was to his friend, Hermie.

Tapping Danny on the shoulder, they both walked to the pro shop to register. They dropped their clubs outside the pro shop and went in. Harvey, the assistant pro, greeted them, "Good morning. It's going to be a great day for golf. How can I help you two?"

"Good morning. I'm Danny Wilson and this is my father. We're here to play in the club championship." Danny told him.

"Well Danny lets see." Harvey said. "You tee off at eight twenty with Max Blackburn and Mark Anderson. Your dad tees off at eight fifty with James Jones and Billy Vickers. Here are your scorecards and pencils. Enjoy your round of golf and hit it straight but not too many times." Danny picked up two small buckets of practice balls from Harvey for his father and himself and off they went.

They spent about fifty minutes on the practice range. The club championship brought out all the good players. They were all busy on the range and putting green. The club championship is contested over only one round. There would be forty-eight players competing for the title. Jim Jackson, the defending champion and previous owner of Bernie, was on the practice area getting ready for his tee time. Danny and his father worked on their swings on the range. Then it was off to the putting green for some fine tuning of the putting stroke. Fifteen minutes later Danny was ready for his tee time.

Danny wished his father, "Good luck."

His father reciprocated, "Play well, son. Do you have enough money for something to drink and eat at the break? I'll see you when we're finished."

Danny told his father he had enough money and walked over towards the first tee. There he introduced himself to his fellow competitors and the starter, "Hi. I'm Danny Wilson."

"Hi, Danny. I'm Max and this is Mark." The players then shook hands and exchanged scorecards. It is a standard rule in all tournaments that competitors keep each others score.

Richard, the starter then announced, "Now on the tee the eight twenty tee time. Up first Mr. Max Blackburn." Max hit his tee shot straight down the middle of the fairway. The starter then announced, "Now on the tee Mr. Mark Anderson." Mark hit his tee shot down the right side of the fairway just barely into the rough. Finally, the starter announced, "Now on the tee our youngest competitor in the club championship, Mr. Danny Wilson."

Danny already had Bernie and a wooden tee in his hand. A little nervous he placed Bernie on the tee. Bernie braced himself for impact and thought, "Here I go off into the wild blue yonder. It's good to back on the course and used again." With a few practice swings and a deep breath, Danny launched Bernie into the air. Bernie flew high over the course and he could see all around. He landed in the middle of the fairway where he rolled a little bit farther. His first trip was over with many more to come. It was a good start for

Danny and Bernie. After Danny hit the ball, he turned to his father and gave him a thumbs up.

In the middle of the fairway Bernie listened to the birds sing and the wind blowing through the trees. The trees made him think of the long time he had been lost in the woods. I also made him think about things he missed a lot like Hermie. He really wondered where his friend was and if he was all right.

Danny arrived where Bernie was lying in the fairway. Hitting the shortest of the three drives, Danny would be hitting first. With confidence a few practice swings and a deep breath, Danny launched Bernie towards the green. He landed on the back fringe but spun backwards to where he finished less than ten feet from the cup. It was a great shot and beginning for Danny.

Max and Mark hit their second shots inside of Danny. Danny would be putting first. Danny marked Bernie with a coin and cleaned off all the dirt carefully. Danny lined up his putt what seemed rather quickly and prepared to putt. He replaced Bernie with the coin and after a few practice strokes was ready. His stroke was jerky, not like on the putting green, so Bernie bounced instead of rolling smoothly. It was probably due to anxiousness or jitters but Bernie missed to the right of the cup. Danny tapped him in for his par. Max and Mark also missed their short birdie putts so all three players had to settle for pars.

The second hole was a long par five hole. It would take two well-struck shots to reach the green in two. All three players hit their tee shots well with only Max finding the edge of the rough. With the distance the tee shots went, all three players would be in that zone to decide whether or not to go for the green in two.

With the balls somewhat close together it gave Bernie a chance to talk to the other balls. "Hi. My name is Bernie. What's yours?"

One of the balls answered, "My name is Jud and that's Jasper. We're both Axiom balls while I see you you're an Excel ball."

Bernie told him, "Yeah! Danny found me in the woods off the ninth hole. I'm just glad to be back on the course again. Well, here come the players. Maybe we can talk some more later."

With the shortest tee shot Danny would have to make the decision whether to go for the green first. Danny was always an aggressive player and like to take chances. With little hesitation he pulled his three wood out of the bag. After a few practice swings and a deep breath Bernie was flying through the air. Bernie flew over all the water and landed safely on dry land. He was a little short of the green but at least he wasn't swimming. Both Danny and especially Bernie breathed a big sigh of relief.

Max and Mark decided not to go for the green and laid up short of the water. Jud and Jasper were relieved Max and Mark played it safe. They would have easy pitches for their next shot. Soon they were where Jud and Jasper were laying. Playing their short pitches, they landed on the green some ten and fifteen feet away respectively from the cup. It was now time for Danny to execute his delicate chip. With a professional like touch, Danny executed a nearly perfect chip shot. It rolled just like a putt and finished less than a foot from the cup. Danny would have a tap-in birdie.

"Great shot and good birdie, Danny." both Max and Mark said as they clapped their hands.

"Thanks. I just got lucky." Danny told them.

Max was able to make his putt for birdie. Mark wasn't as lucky. He lipped out both his first and second putts. He had to settle for a three putt bogey. Even with Mark making bogey the group walked to the next tee with smiles on their faces. Max would tee off first with Danny second and Mark third.

Max hit his tee shot straight down the middle of the fairway. Danny launched Bernie off the tee next. Danny seemed to rush the swing and Bernie veered to the right into the woods. He hit one of the trees and dropped straight down. This made Bernie extremely nervous. It made him recall being lost before. Mark hit tee shot down the middle like Max but not as far.

After what seemed an eternity to Bernie, Danny arrived at where Bernie was in the trees. Bernie breathed a sigh of relief. Danny was facing a challenging shot ahead. He would have to thread the ball between the trees and over a bunker to get to the green. Danny spent a little extra time planning out his strategy. One of the big differences in the club championship to a pro tournament is that players have the option of using a caddie or not, in certain situations it's nice to have someone to confer with. Finally, when Danny was ready he took a few practice swings, a deep breath and launched Bernie through the narrow opening in the trees. He whistled past the leaves and branches. Bernie bounced once in the fairway and plopped into the sand trap. Bernie was half buried in the sand but at least he was away from the trees.

Mark congratulated Danny on the good shot out of the trees. Danny told him, "I just got lucky and chose the right opening." Max and Mark both hit their second shots onto the green within birdie range. Soon, Danny was up to where his ball laid in the sand trap. He noticed it was half buried and it would call for an explosion shot. He stepped down into the sand and dug his feet into the sand. With a steep upright swing Bernie popped right out of the sand onto the green. He finished some fifteen feet from the cup. Danny would still have a chance to make par.

Mark putted first and missed his birdie chance just to the right. Next to putt was Danny. He lined up his putt from all four sides and was determined to make it. A few practice strokes and Bernie was on his way. He broke more than Danny had allowed and missed to the right. Danny raised his arms in disgust and quickly tapped Bernie in for his bogey. Danny would have to forget he made a bogey. He had to remember there were a lot more holes to play. Max missed his birdie putt as well so he and Mark would have to settle for pars. Danny would be teeing off last on the next hole. It would give him some time to calm down and think.

On the next four holes, all three of the golfers made routine uneventful pars. So far after seven holes Max was one under, Danny was even and Mark was one over par. After the par three eighth hole this would change. The eighth hole is a short tricky par three hole. The player needed to negotiate a large trap in front and a small pond. Going for the green was no bargain either, with a steep embankment making a pitch shot very difficult.

Max hit his tee shot first. This was the water that Jud had been lost in. When he landed on the green, Jud was relieved. He didn't stay on the green but rolled down the steep embankment in back. Mark then hit Jasper short into the sand trap, where he was buried. After these two tee shots, Danny had some uncertainty in his thoughts on what club to use. He placed Bernie on a tee and decided on a club. With more practice swings than normal, Danny launched Bernie into the air.

Bernie flew over the pond and sand trap. He landed on the green with such impact the he made a large divot and spun backwards. He finished some fifteen feet from the cup. Danny had executed a well thought out shot. Bernie was very proud of him.

Max and Mark made reasonable recovery shots from their precarious situations. They both would have reasonable putts for pars. Danny arrived where Bernie had stopped. He first marked him with a coin, repaired the divot on the green and cleaned him off. Mark, who putted first, made his double breaking putt for a hard working par. Danny, putting next, selected his line and remarked Bernie. With a few practice strokes Bernie was on his way towards the cup. Danny had figured the line correctly and Bernie fell right into the cup. It was one of the better strokes of the round so far that Danny had made. Max lipped out his putt for par and had to settle for bogey.

On the ninth tee there was a delay. The group ahead had lost a ball in the woods on the left. The players rested on the bench while on the tee. Their balls were on the ground in front of them, which gave them a chance to talk. Bernie told the other two, "This was the hole where I got lost. I was in the woods for a long time till Danny found me."

Jasper told Bernie, "This is where I got lost also. I was there over two months till someone accidentally stepped on me. They picked me up and I was bought later by Mark in the pro shop. Jud told both of them, "I got lucky. I was fished from the water on the last hole. I was then bought later by Max in the pro shop as well."

Bernie then said, "Well, it looks like all three of us have had rocky roads. I'm also looking for a friend of mine. We were made in the same factory and got very close."

Jasper asked, "When did you see him last?"

Bernie told him, "Just before I was bought in the pro shop."

Jud said, "You're going to be lucky if you ever see him again. Your chances are astronomical."

Bernie firmly told him, "I still have faith we will meet again. You have to believe and always have hope. Some things have a way of working out."

It was about time for the players to tee off. Danny, teeing off first, put Bernie on a tee. Bernie had beads of sweat running over his cover and his rubber bands were pulsating inside him. Danny took a deep breath, a few practice swings, and launched Bernie into the air. Bernie flew straight as an arrow down the middle of the fairway. Jud and Jasper flew straight down the middle as well. They almost seem to stick their tongues out at the trees. What a relief to all three of them!

All three of the balls were ready for their second shots and anxious to get this hole over with. Danny had hit the farthest tee shot so he would be hitting last. Max hit Jud first and he finished some two feet behind the cup. Mark hit Jasper next about two feet to the right of the cup. Now it was time for Danny. Danny launched Bernie into the air. He flew so straight at the pin that he wrapped inside the flag. A few seconds later he dropped straight down about three inches from the cup. All three players were giving each other high fives all the way down the fairway for their great shots. They all had gimmie birdies. It was sweet revenge for the three players and the three balls.

A short time later all three players tapped their birdie putts into the cup. Danny had finished the front nine two under par. Max and Mark finished one under and even, respectively. All three golfers walked off the ninth green with smiles on their faces. Danny said, "That was fun and cool." Max and Mark agreed. Bernie, Jud and Jasper also had smiles on their faces.

CHAPTER 13

A Nine to Remember

The first nine was over so Danny put Bernie in his pocket. Together the players went into the clubhouse to get a snack and something to drink. A short while later they emerged ready to play the back nine. It was then that Danny saw his father who was just finishing his front nine. He went over to see him.

Danny asked, "How did it go dad?" I shot two under. I made great birdies on the last two holes."

His father answered, "That's great, son. I shot two over and lost a ball in the water on number eight. I'm glad you played well. Keep it going on the back nine and we'll celebrate when you're finished. Are you still using that Excel ball you found?"

"I sure am. It's my good luck charm. I plan to use it the entire round. Talk to you when you're finished. Time for me to tee off." With that Danny hugged his father and walked over to the tenth tee where the other two players were waiting.

The second nine begins with a relatively easy par four. It's straight away and with two good shots a birdie would be a good possibility. With birdies on both the eighth and ninth holes Danny would have the honors. A few extra practice swings and Bernie was on his way. He landed right in the middle of the fairway. Max and Mark hit good tee shots as well but short of Danny. All three players would have simple approach shots to the green.

On their second shots Jud and Jasper landed on the green in definite birdie range. Bernie on the other hand finished twenty feet from the cup. It wasn't a very accurate second shot by Danny.

Bernie blurted out to the other balls, "At least the players are still using all of us." The other two balls winked at Bernie as they waited patiently till the players arrived. Danny arrived first and marked Bernie with a coin. As he cleaned Bernie off he muttered to himself, "That sure wasn't a very accurate shot I hit." Bernie felt like saying to him, "Make it up with a well stroked putt."

Danny replaced Bernie where the coin was. He lined Bernie up from all four sides and figured he had a good idea of the correct line. A few practice strokes and Bernie was on his way. He rolled smoothly over the contour of the green but broke more to the right than Danny had allowed. He finished right on the lip of the cup. If a slight breeze were to come up, it would cause him to fall into the cup. With no breeze coming, Danny tapped Bernie into the cup for a par. Mark made his birdie putt but Max missed his just to the left.

Walking over to the next tee Danny would be teeing off second with Mark being first. The eleventh hole at the Ambassador Country Club is a short par five but has trouble everywhere. The trouble starts with a large lake on the right side. There's out of bounds all the way up to the green along the left side. Fairway and greenside sand traps also are strategically placed. It demands two accurate well thought out shots. Danny looked over his shoulder to see that his father had hit his tee shot on number ten in the middle of the fairway.

Mark, with the honors, hit his tee shot well but it headed right towards the water. Jasper got nervous as the water neared. The other two balls on the tee closed their eyes to hope and pray for Jasper. He hit just short of the water but trickled into the edge. Covered halfway with water and hidden by some reeds, Jasper just hoped Mark would find him.

It was time for Danny to tee off now. He placed Bernie on a tee. Bernie was nervous after seeing what had happened to Jasper. Danny took a deep breath, a few extra practice swings and Bernie was launched into the air. He flew high over the trees and landed on the edge of the fairway. He rolled another twenty yards before stopping just short of the fairway trap. Bernie figured Danny had hit his tee shot far enough to go for the green in two.

Max was up last. He hit the worst tee shot of the group. He hooked Jud left into the trees, which then ricocheted out of bounds. Hitting another ball off the tee due to the penalty, he hooked this one as well into the woods but luckily not out of bounds. Max and mark walked off the tee with a disgusted look on their faces and mumbling to themselves.

Max got to his ball in the woods first. He didn't bother looking for the first ball, Jud, for he was far into the trees. The other ball was stymied next to a tree. He would have to take an unplayable lie. According to the rules of golf, the ball is dropped not nearer the hole incurring a one stroke penalty. On his next shot he was able to advance the ball up the fairway almost to the water. He was laying five. Jud was now gone, lost in the woods.

Mark was now up to where Jasper laid in the water. Thankfully, he found him almost right away. He decided to extricate Jasper from the water instead of taking an unplayable. He was able to pitch Jasper out of the water like a sand explosion shot. He didn't go far but Mark still might be able to reach the green in regulation. Meanwhile, Danny patiently sat on the edge of his golf bag watching and thinking about his next shot.

Bernie knew that Jud was lost when he saw a new ball lying where Max had hit. Jasper, a little ways in front of Bernie, probably realized it as well. Bernie sure wished he could talk to Danny. He would like to ask him if he knew any other Excel balls outside of himself and Arturo? He would also tell Danny to go for the green in two. He had confidence in him.

When it was time for Danny to play, he had firmly decided to go for the green in two. A deep breath, a few practice swings and Bernie was flying over the water towards the green. Danny had hit him well but he barely cleared the water. He finished on the edge of the green some thirty feet from the cup. Danny would have a challenging but makable eagle putt.

Max and Mark played their approach shots. All three players weren't talking much walking up to the green. Max, after going out of bounds and suffering an unplayable, laid six on the green about ten feet from the cup. Mark had air mailed his third shot over the green. A great pitch shot left him about eight feet for par. Penalty strokes and mistakes frustrated and changed the complete demeanor of Max and Mark.

Danny on the other hand felt great and was able to mark Bernie with a coin. He couldn't let the distractions of the troubles the other players were having distract him. He cleaned off Bernie and lined up the putt carefully. He stroked the putt confidently. Bernie rolled over and over towards the cup but stopped on the lip of the cup but only for a second. Plunk!! into the cup Bernie fell. It was an eagle!!! Danny leaped into the air with joy and went, "You betcha!!!!"

Max and Mark clapped their hands in approval and said, "Way to go, Danny."

Before Max putted, Jasper and Bernie realized now for sure that Jud was gone. Max missed his putt and had to settle for a triple bogey eight. Max was so disgusted that he threw his ball right into the water. It shocked both Jasper and Bernie. Mark had no luck either in his putting. He lipped out both the first and second putts and had to settle for a double bogey seven.

Danny was in high spirits. The other two players on the other hand were grumbling to themselves as they walked. When they got to the tee, Max opened the pocket of his golf bag and pulled out another ball. Jasper was done as well.

Mark put him in his golf bag and pulled out another. Jud was now gone. Jasper was retired. Bernie was the only one left of the original three.

For the next few holes the players were quiet and went about their business. Hitting fairways and greens was the name of the game. All three players did this and made routine pars over the next three holes. Bernie on the other hand was busy trying to make new friends. The two new balls were Axiom balls. Their names were Artie and Shelby.

The fifteenth hole was a par three measuring one hundred and sixty-five yards. It was completely over water. It demanded a correct choice in club and commitment. Selecting what he thought would be the perfect club, Danny took a deep breath and a few extra practice swings. He launched Bernie over the water towards the green. Bernie flew high and straight and just cleared the water. He finished in some deep grass in front of the green. Max and Mark both were able to hit their tee shots onto the green in perfect position.

Bernie, while waiting for Danny, could see his own reflection in the water. It brought back memories of his friend Hermie and how much he missed him. When Danny arrived, he realized how lucky he was in missing the water. It would require an unorthodox stance and swing to extricate Bernie from the deep grass. A steep upright swing made Bernie nervous. That kind of swing could easily pop him back into the water.

Danny stood looking into the water at his reflection. He was in deep, deep thought. Reflecting enough, he decided on his course of action. He assumed an awkward stance with one foot in the edge of the water. Unable to ground his club, he took a very upright swing. Bernie popped out of the grass like a cork out of a bottle. He landed on the fringe of the green and stopped right there.

"Well played, Danny. Your father would be proud." said Mark.

"Thank you." replied Danny as he mumbled to himself. "Now if I can make this putt."

Bernie wanted to congratulate Danny too. Under the rules of golf Danny couldn't mark Bernie so he couldn't be cleaned. Bernie had mud all over him. Danny would have a difficult time putting especially controlling direction. Danny took his time and made the best stroke he could. Bernie because of the mud, rolled unsteadily. He finished some three feet to the right of the cup. It was a good putt considering. Danny marked Bernie with a coin, cleaned him off and waited till it was his turn again. Max and Mark both made their putts for birdies. Shortly after that Danny rather nonchalantly tapped Bernie into the cup. It was a bogey for Danny but it could have been much worse.

Danny was disappointed with the bogey and would be teeing off last. Both Max and Mark tried to keep Danny positive by telling him he was still playing a great round of golf. This brought a smile to his face. It also made Bernie feel good. Danny needed some positive vibes. The next hole required all his attention.

There was a small logjam on the tee. A player in the group ahead had lost a ball in the water. The sixteenth hole at the Ambassador Country Club was the most scenic and picturesque. It was featured on the front of the scorecard and shown in numerous golf magazines. A short par four of two hundred and ninety-five yards, it demanded cutting across the water to reach the green in one. Most players took the conservative route but some did take the gamble.

Bernie looked over at Artie and said, "I wonder if any of the players will go for the green?"

Artie answered, "All I hope is that we all see each other on the green."

"That goes ditto for me." reiterated Shelby.

The question was about to be answered. Being up first Max was going for the green. He launched Shelby across the water but fell just short and splashed into the water. Mark was going at the green as well and Artie was shivering in nervousness. He hit Artie into the sand trap guarding the green. "Whew!!" Artie thought as he avoided the water. After the last two tee shots would Danny still go for the green. Bernie wondered.

Danny, still a little upset with himself over the last hole, was going for the green anyway. A few practice swings and Bernie was launched like he was shot out of a rifle. Bernie skipped across the water and finished scared but dry on the fringe of the green. It was exhilarating but nerve racking.

Taking his penalty stroke, Max hit his next shot onto the green from the penalty drop area. A par was still possible. Mark and Danny walked together towards the green. Mark said to Danny, "I really like playing in this club championship. I have especially enjoyed playing with you. You're quite a golfer for your age and fun to watch."

Danny told him, "It has been fun playing with you as well. I've really enjoyed the competition and hope we can play together again." With that the players arrived where their ball were lying.

Mark had a difficult shot from the sand trap. His ball was lying under the lip of the trap. After a few practice swings outside the trap, he assumed his stance, digging his feet into the sand. Mark exploded Artie out of the trap. He landed on the far fringe and stopped. If he had rolled a few more inches, he would have been in the water. Artie breathed a sigh of relief and Bernie was thankful for him.

Max fished Shelby from out of the water and put him in his golf bag. He was done for the day and probably off to the shag bag. Bernie really never did get to know him. Danny got ready to stroke Bernie. On the fringe Danny wasn't allowed to clean Bernie and there was a large clump of mud on him. It would be hard to control the shot. It was a like a putt he had on the eighth hole. Danny stroked Bernie as well as he could. Bernie rolled unsteadily and finished some two feet from the cup. It was a good effort concerning the circumstances. Marking Bernie and cleaning him off, Danny decided to finish and tapped Bernie into the center of the cup. It was a birdie and Danny was back to four under par for the tournament. Looking at a nearby scoreboard, he then realized he was tied for the lead with ironically, Jim Jackson. Even after going in the water Max was still able to get his par. Mark also only made par lipping out his birdie try.

Danny would have the honors on the seventeenth tee. This hole was a straightaway par four with numerous sand traps including the largest one on the course. The main challenge though was an undulating green that broke numerous directions. All three players hit their tee shots straight down the middle of the fairway with Danny driving the farthest.

Bernie listened to the birds chirping away as he waited for Danny. It gave Bernie a chance to talk to Artie and meet the new ball. Bernie said, "How are you doing, Artie? It's too bad about Shelby and the water. Who's the new ball?"

Artie told Bernie, "I'm doing fine. At least Shelby was found and hopefully will get used again. The new ball is Josh and he's really quiet and shy. He was used before and lost in the woods for over two months. Should sound familiar to you Bernie."

Bernie told him, "Yes, that does bring back some unpleasant memories. At least I can say, Hi. Nice to meet you, Josh. I'm Bernie."

"Hello." Josh said very softly. "I don't think we will get to talk much more considering it is almost the end of the round."

Danny arrived where Bernie was lying in the fairway. Max and Mark had hit their shots within birdie range on the green. Taking what seemed a very short time, Danny selected a club and launched Bernie towards the green. Rushing as he did Bernie finished on the green but some forty feet from the pin. It was one of the worst iron shots Danny had hit all day. The nerves of playing in a tournament and in contention had come into play. Danny would now face the immense pressure of a long double breaking putt. It was a putt not easy under any circumstances. Bernie just hoped and prayed Danny would be up to the task.

Spectators completely surrounded the back of the green and greeted the players with a nice applause when they arrived. Danny repaired his ball mark, marked Bernie and cleaned him off. He gave Bernie a little smack with his lips and mumbled as if talking to him. Danny took a little extra time lining Bernie up. When he was ready, he took a few practice strokes and Bernie was rolling. He rolled to the right and then to the left before stopping just short of the cup. It was a great lag putt by Danny. The people acknowledged his effort with a nice applause. Danny tapped Bernie in for his par and raised his putter into the air thanking the people for the applause. While waiting for Max and Mark to putt, Danny took a quick glance at the scoreboard near the green and saw he was still tied for the lead. Bernie tried to peek as well. Max and Mark both made their birdie putts and received a nice applause from the excited crowd.

All three players walked through the crowd to the eighteenth tee. As they walked people patted them on their backs and wished them good luck. The fairway was lined with spectators from the tee to the green. There was tension and excitement in the air. Most of that tension rested on the shoulders of young Danny.

The finishing hole at the Ambassador Country Club was a great par five hole and a stern test of golf. It demanded accuracy off the tee and a well-played second. Trees guarded the right side of the fairway while a large lake guarded the left. The green presented its own challenge. It was the largest on the course covering almost an acre. It had undulations breaking to the right and left everywhere. It was a great finishing hole for any round of golf.

Max hit his tee shot first and it ended up on the edge of the right rough. Mark, hitting next, pushed his tee shot a little farther right than Max and could have some tree trouble. Then it was time for Danny. With some noticeable nervousness he placed Bernie on the tee. Danny went to his bag and dried off his hands.

Someone from out of the crowd yelled, "Hit it straight and solid, Danny." Danny just nodded his head and with his one wood in hand walked back over towards Bernie. After a few extra practice swings and a deep breath, Danny sent Bernie flying through the air. He landed in the middle of the fairway but hit a mound and took a hard bounce to the left. He stopped in the fairway just short of the large lake. Applause could be heard all over the golf course. It was a good pressure tee shot Danny had produced. Bernie couldn't talk to the other balls for they were on the other side of the fairway. He sure wished Hermie were around to have someone to share his excitement with.

Waiting for Danny, Bernie could hear the spectators mumbling. Soon, Danny arrived where Bernie was lying. He looked over to the other two players and realized he would be hitting his second shot last. Knowing that, he sat down on the edge of his golf bag looking at Bernie. He seemed to wish Bernie would tell him which way to go. He was also thinking about his father and what he would do.

Finally, Danny stood up and took a deep breath. He had been aggressive all day and this was no time to change. Danny selected a three wood from his bag and began his preparation. A few extra practice swings and a deep breath and he was ready. Bernie flew through the air over the water. He veered slightly to the right and finished in a greenside sand trap. The trap shot wouldn't be difficult, only the circumstances.

Mark had to chip out of the trees. A big oak stymied him. He managed to get his next shot on the green. He would still have a putt for birdie from over forty feet. Max hit his second shot about seventy yards short of the green. He would have an easy pitch for his third. Max hit his third onto the green but about thirty feet from the cup.

Danny arrived at the greenside bunker. He had an uphill lie and at least the ball wasn't buried. Danny popped Bernie right out of the trap but he didn't hit him hard enough. Bernie finished some forty-five feet from the cup. Danny would be putting first on the tricky green.

All three players walked onto the green to a nice applause from the gallery. Danny marked Bernie with a coin. He cleaned him off and put him to his lips. Danny whispered to Bernie, "I need a good putt." With that he gave Bernie a small kiss and remarked him. He lined up the putt from all four sides and took a little extra time studying the grass around the cup. Maybe it was telepathy from Bernie to check the grain of the grass.

Danny gave Bernie a firm rap and he was on his way. He bounced at first but rolled smoothly over the hills and valleys of the green. As he approached the cup, the gallery let out a gasp thinking the putt would miss to the right. Bernie stopped though right on the lip of the cup. Plunk!! It was a birdie! Danny leaped and threw his putter into the air. The crowd applauded loudly as Danny walked towards the cup. Danny pulled Bernie from the cup and gave him a big smack. It seemed like Bernie turned a little red from embarrassment.

Mark, after the applause calmed down, missed his birdie putt and had to settle for par. Max missed as well but salvaged par. The round was over and the three players traded handshakes. Off to the scorers' tent the three players went.

Danny entered first and sat down in the middle chair. There he carefully and methodically checked and rechecked his scorecard. He signed his card and witnessed the other two cards. He was done and it was official. The scorer then said to Danny, "Congratulations young man. You are tied for the tournament lead." With that Danny shook his hand and left.

Outside the tent many people congratulated Danny on his round. Danny said, "Thanks, Max and Mark. I look forward to when we can play again."

"Good luck to you too, Danny. Hope you win the tournament. You played great." Mark and Max told him.

Danny then walked over to the eighteenth green where his father was finishing. He had Bernie neatly tucked away in his pocket. His father had just finished when Danny got to the green. He hugged his dad and walked with him towards the scorers' tent.

Danny waited outside while his dad verified his score. His dad had shot even par which was a great round for him. When he came out he put his arm around Danny and they walked to the eighteenth green to see the last players come in. One of those players was Jim Jackson. He was the player Danny was tied with for the title.

Danny asked his father, "How did your round go?" You can tell by the big scoreboard how well I did."

"I'm very proud of you Danny. You did absolutely great." his father told him. "I shot even par which was a great round for me."

"Lets now watch Mr. Jackson finish and see if there will be a playoff or not." Danny told his father. With that the two of them watched the proceedings on the green.

CHAPTER 14
The Playoff

On the eighteenth green Mr. Jackson was just getting ready to putt. He had reached the par five hole in two. Jim had just bogeyed the last hole and needed two putts to tie Danny. Peeking out of the pocket, Bernie could see the green and where the ball was laying. He thought he recognized the ball Jim was using. He thought it might be Cal. Jim spent quite a while lining up his putt. The putt measured well over sixty feet.

The putt was soon rolling across the green. It stopped some seven feet short of the cup. It was a good effort by Jim considering the circumstances.

Danny turned to his father and said, "I better get started warming up."

His father answered, "Wait, we have time to watch him finish. Danny decided to wait, which made Bernie glad. Jim Jim lined up his putt carefully and rammed it right into the back of the cup. The crowd erupted in giant applause. Jim pulled his ball from the cup and raised his putter in celebration. There would be a playoff to determine the club champion.

The playoff would start at the first hole. It would begin about thirty minutes after Jim finalized his scorecard and rested a bit. Danny went straight over to the putting green and was getting ready with his father. His father was going to caddie for him in the playoff. One of the longtime members of the club offered to carry the other bag.

Danny was asked by his father, "What ball do you want to use? The one you were using seems pretty scuffed up."

Danny answered him, "The ball has been great the entire round. No reason to change my luck now." Bernie was relieved when he heard Danny. It made him proud and ready to perform.

A crowd was gathering around the first tee. The two players met at the tee and shook hands. Jim and Danny had never played together before. Danny told Jim, "I'll be using an Excel one." Jim told Danny, "I'll be using a Perennial six." Bernie didn't know the other ball but hoped to get to talk to him during the playoff.

Mr. Abraham, the president of the club, flipped a coin to determine who had honors. Danny said, "Heads." It was tails. Jim would have the honors to start the playoff.

Jim hit his tee shot straight down the middle of the fairway and received a nice applause. Danny, up next, placed Bernie on a tee and using his one wood smacked him right down the center of the fairway almost up to where the other ball lay. Over a thousand spectators followed the twosome off the tee to watch.

Bernie laying by the other ball whispered, "Hi. My name is Bernie. Pretty exciting isn't it?"

The other ball answered, "Hi, Bernie. My name Artemis. This is my first action ever on a golf course. I'm really nervous. I've heard a lot of rumors from other golf balls."

Bernie told him, "Calm down, everything will be alright. We'll talk more later, hopefully."

Jim and Danny arrived at where the balls were lying. Danny would be up first. His father handed Danny a club from the bag. Danny and his father had played together numerous times and knew each others game like the back of their hand. Danny told his father, "Thanks, Dad. I'm glad you're here with me." With that said, Danny hit a perfect iron shot, which finished some seven feet from the pin. Jim hit a good shot as well but outside Danny. Jim would be putting first.

Arriving at the green the players received a nice applause from the crowd. Both players repaired their divots and marked their balls with coins. Jim, putting first, lined his putt up and with a firm stroke knocked his ball right into the back of the cup. Danny applauded, recognizing the good putt. He then remarked Bernie and whispered to him, "We need this putt." With a perfect stroke Bernie rolled right into the center of the cup. The playoff was still tied so it was over to the tough par five second hole.

During the regular round, both Jim and Danny had birdied the par five second. Jim, teeing off first, hit Artemis straight down the middle of the fairway. Danny hit Bernie straight down the middle as well but not as far as Jim. Both tee shots though, were far enough to go for the green in two.

Talking and walking to his ball, Danny and his father decided not to go for the green but lay up for an easy pitch. Jim took the aggressive path. He went for the green and was applauded by the crowd. He was also rewarded with a makeable eagle putt.

Danny and his father arrived at where Bernie was. Danny was about seventy yards short of the putting surface and an additional forty feet to the pin. Danny selected his pitching wedge and asked his father, "What do you think?"

His father told him, "Make a confident shot and visualize it. I have confidence in you."

With that said, Danny took a few practice swings and made a smooth swing. Bernie bounced about ten feet in front of the cup and trickled right in. It was an eagle!!! and a great shot under pressure. The crowd erupted into a deafening applause.

Danny proudly walked onto the green. Jim shook his hand saying, "Great shot, Danny." Danny then pulled Bernie out of the cup and gave him a big smooch on the cover. Bernie almost seemed to turn red. Jim would now face his twenty foot putt just to tie Danny. He lined it up carefully and with a confident stroke putted the ball right into the back of the cup. The crowd erupted again into a deafening applause. The amazing playoff would continue at least one more hole.

Jim and Danny both hit their tee shots in the fairway about the same distance on the next hole. One of the officials watching the match would have to decide who was furthest away. Bernie looked over at Artemis and said, "This sure is exciting with the shotmaking and the crowds."

Artemis asked Bernie, "Are rounds of golf always this hectic and nerve racking?"

Bernie told him, "So far every round I have been a part of has had its share of excitement."

The official decided that Jim was further away. Jim selected his club. He hit his shot short of the green where it finished in the deep grass just short of the fringe. Danny launched Bernie at the green where he finished some thirty feet from the cup. An inaccurate shot but good under the circumstances. The crowd applauded both the players for the great competition they were having.

Jim, when he saw his lie, shook his head. His shot called for a perfectly executed flop shot. Jim played an average shot where Artemis finished some ten feet from the cup. He would face a difficult ten foot putt to save par.

While Jim was playing his flop shot, Danny was busy lining up Bernie for his putt. He and his father concurred and agreed on the appropriate line. Danny hit a few practice strokes and Bernie was on his way. They had figured the line correctly but Danny hadn't hit the putt hard enough. The ball stopped some four feet short. Danny marked Bernie where he had finished and decided to putt out. He knocked his second putt right into the back of the cup.

Danny had his par and now Jim needed to make his putt. He spent longer than usual lining the putt up. He stroked it firmly and it dropped right into the center of the cup. The crowd applauded its approval of both players play. The playoff would continue on.

The fourth hole was a demanding par four. Jim, up first, hit his tee shot solid but it bounced into the thick rough on the right side of the fairway. Danny hit his tee shot straight down the middle about the same distance. The crowd had swelled to over two thousand spectators. The players and their caddies walked together down the fairway.

Jim arrived where Artemis had settled down into the rough. He was down there deeply snarled amongst the tall grass. Jim selected his club and with a strong swing Artemis flew like a bullet out of the grass. He landed short of the green but rolled all the way to the back fringe. He was some forty feet away from the cup.

Danny hit his second shot right onto the green about fifteen feet to the right of the cup. He would have a makeable birdie putt. Both players received a nice applause from the huge crowd. They had witnessed a great playoff so far.

At the green Jim was unable to mark his ball being on the fringe of the green. There was a large clump of mud on the ball but Jim would have to negotiate the putt as best he could. He knew how important this putt was so he spent a little extra time lining it up. Finally, when he was ready, he stroked the putt as best he could. Artemis finished about seven feet short of the cup. Danny would now have a putt to win the playoff.

Danny and his father whispered to one another about the approximate line. Danny then whispered to Bernie, "If I ever needed a putt, this is the one." With that said, Danny remarked Bernie and prepared to putt. He stroked the putt on his intended line but it just missed to the right. Danny tapped in the remainder to get his par.

Jim now had his seven-foot downhill putt to tie. The crowd was so quiet you could hear a pin drop. Jim stroked the putt firmly but too firmly. It caught the edge of the cup and rimmed out. The playoff was over and Danny was the club champion. Jim went over to Danny and shook his hand in congratulations. The ending of the playoff was somewhat anticlimactic after the great shotmaking. The crowd applauded the players as Danny hugged his father.

Mr. Abraham then approached Danny and told him, "Please walk with me back to the clubhouse for the awards ceremony. Congratulations, Danny." The players, caddies and the crowd all proceeded back towards the clubhouse.

CHAPTER 15

The Reunion

The playoff was over and Danny was the club champion. The players along with Mr. Abraham walked back to the clubhouse. The crowd that had been watching the playoff followed behind. While walking back, various people offering congratulations approached Danny. Danny got a special big hug from his dad.

Mr. Abraham came over to Danny and Jim, "That was an amazing playoff you two had. It will be remembered here at the club for many years. We'll be holding a short award ceremony on the eighteenth green. See you both there."

Danny kept getting congratulations from various members. Jim, the good sportsman that he was, had his arm around Danny. Soon, both saw Mr. Hart and Mr. Jacobs bringing out a table for the ceremony. It was time to meet at the green.

Mr. Abraham began the festivities. He announced,

"Welcome to the award ceremony for the newly crowned club champion. We witnessed some great rounds of competitive golf, which culminated with an unbelievable playoff. I salute all the competitors for their great play." A loud applause interrupted him as he continued, "We're proud here at the Ambassador Country Club to recognize, Danny Wilson, as the new club champion. We would also like to recognize, Jim Jackson, the defending champion, who put up such a valiant effort in defending his title." A loud applause again interrupted Mr. Abraham as the players approached.

Danny approached Mr. Abraham where he shook his hand and was handed the club champion trophy. Mr. Abraham then stated, "Danny Wilson is the youngest club champion in the fifty year history of our great club. Danny would you please say a few words."

With trophy in hand Danny approached the microphone. He said, "I want to thank everyone who attended today. Your support really helped me. I want to especially thank Mr. Jackson for the great playoff, my father and all the members of the club. I look forward to next year to come back and defend my title." With that said, Danny shook the hand of Mr. Jackson, Mr. Hart, Mr. Jacobs and Mr. Abraham. The ceremony was over and the crowd dispersed.

Mr. Abraham then took Danny to one side and told him, "I need to talk to you in my office for a few minutes. Your dad should come as well."

Danny told him, "Sure, I'll go get my dad."

All three along with Mr. Hart walked over to his office in the clubhouse. They sat down and made themselves comfortable. Mr. Abraham began, "Congratulations again, Danny. As you've seen there is a large display case in the rotunda. It shows accomplishments here at the club. I would like to display your trophy, a copy of your scorecard and one of the balls you used. A plaque would explain the date and playoff you and Jim had. It would be on display where all people could recognize your winning of the championship."

Danny told him, "It would be an honor. I have the golf ball I used the complete time in the tournament in my pocket." He handed Bernie to Mr. Hart who would take care of it until the plaque was done and the ceremony took place. Mr. Abraham told Danny and his father, "I'll contact you when things are ready."

Bernie realized that he would probably never be used on a golf course again. He also realized that his search for his friend, Hermie, would never materialize. Bernie would miss Danny and the excitement of the golf course. Such was the life of a golf ball, always filled with uncertainty.

Danny gave the ball and trophy to Mr. Hart. He went back to the pro shop where he put them on a shelf in the closet. Bernie was back at the place where his life had started at the Ambassador Country Club. It was getting towards night when Bernie spoke, "Hi. Anyone here in the closet I know. It's Bernie."

A voice came from one of the range buckets. A ball said, "My name is Arthur. A few months ago there was ball in here. He was talking to one of the other range balls. His name was Arnold. The only bad thing was that Arnold was lost about a week ago and hasn't been heard from since."

Bernie asked Arthur, "What was the name of the ball Arnold was talking to?"

Arthur told him, "I think I heard his name was Hermie."

Bernie exuberantly exclaimed, "You're not kidding me are you!! That's my friend I've been looking for since we got separated. What was he doing in here?"

Arthur explained to him, "I don't know why he was here but about two weeks later he was gone again and hasn't been back since."

Two weeks had passed since Danny had won the club championship. Bernie was still all alone on the shelf. That morning he heard voices outside the closet that sounded familiar to him. It was Danny and his father talking to Al. A short time later Al came into the closet and picked up Bernie and the trophy.

Al said, "Lets go over to the rotunda for the ceremony. Mr. Abraham and the other attendees are waiting for us."

With Bernie and the trophy in his hand the three of them walked over to the clubhouse rotunda. Mr. Abraham took the trophy and ball from Al. He placed them on the table with a plaque next to a large wooden glass display case.

Mr. Abraham then announced, "I would like to begin this special ceremony by thanking out new club champion, Danny Wilson. He played a great championship. I would also like to thank Mr. Al Hart and Mr. Harvey Jacobs for holding such a well-organized championship."

Al then opened the display case. He picked up the plaque, scorecard, ball and trophy off the table. Mr. Abraham then called Danny over. He explained to Danny and all in attendance, "Your memorabilia of the championship will be on display for the whole year. We're proud to have you as part of the history of this great club."

Al then handed Danny the trophy. He sat it on its padded pedestal next to the other trophy in the case. In front Danny placed Bernie on the ball stand and the plaque to the right of him. Bernie from his vantage point could read the plaque and at least feel the warm rays of the outdoor sun. Finally, Al tacked up the scorecard above them all.

All in attendance clapped their hands as Al locked the display case. The ceremony was over and all the people left. Bernie had small tears falling from his eyes. He was happy but in the same way sad.

Bernie started looking around his surroundings. To the right was the plaque and trophy. Above them was the scorecard. To the left Bernie got the surprise of his life. Two golf balls sat on stands like his. One of the balls he recognize but the other was a shock. Bernie yelled out vibrating the glass of the display case. "HERMIE!!!!" Hermie looked over and yelled, "BERNIE!!!!" vibrating the glass again. Both balls had tears running from their eyes. The two close friends had found each other in the most unlikely of places.

Bernie said, "Hermie, I sure have missed you. So much has been going on that we have a lot of catching up to do."

Hermie told him, "We have all the time in the world. Neither one of us is going anywhere soon."

The two golf balls sat on their stands staring at one another for hours. The sun shined through the window causing a rainbow on the glass. It was a beautiful ending to a reunion and a great day.